SHARON A. MITCHELL

SANCTUM

VINCI
BOOKS

By Sharon A. Mitchell

When Bad Things Happen

GONE

TRUST

SELFISH

INSTINCT

REASONS WHY

MINE

SANCTUM

Vinci Books

vinci-books.com

Published by Vinci Books Ltd in 2025

1

The publisher and the author have made every effort to obtain permissions for any third party material used in this book and to comply with copyright law. Any queries in this respect should be brought to the attention of the publisher and any omissions will be corrected in future editions.

A CIP catalogue record for this book is available from the British Library.

Paperback ISBN: 9781036707569

The EU GPSR authorised representative is Logos Europe, 9 rue Nicolas Poussion, 17000 La Rochelle, France
contact@logoseurope.eu

Part I

Chapter One

1983

"Are you sure?" Jerry's huge frame supported the two little boys swinging from his outstretched arms. He smiled at the older boy, Alex, as the child shrieked in delight. "Me and the missus can keep the kids, and you can send for them once you're settled."

Olivia agreed. "Jerry and I don't mind at all. We'd love to have them."

Janice shook her head. "Thanks, but no. We'll be fine." She hoped.

"Are you sure that you and what's his name don't need a little bit of time to adjust to the new place, just the two of you?"

"No, we'll tackle the surprise together. And his name is Luke."

"Surprise?" Oh, no, thought Olivia. She eyed Janice steadily. "Luke does know that the three of you are coming, doesn't he?"

Janice looked away. "Maybe not exactly, but it'll be okay.

3

Once he sees the boys, there's not much he can do, is there? I mean, he can't turn us away."

"Oh, Janice, Janice." Jerry ran a hand over his face. "The man doesn't know you have two sons. Really? Are you telling me he expects you to show up alone, that it'll be just the two of you living together?"

Olivia took one of Janice's hands in hers. "Really, the boys will be fine with us if you want to go alone, break the news to this Luke in person, work things out."

"No!" Janice yanked her hand away. "It'll be *fine*, I tell you. It'll all work out. Love me, love my kids, and all that, you know."

Lowering himself to his knees, Jerry let the little boys climb from his arms to his shoulders. With one beefy hand on each child's back, he steadied the two- and four-year-olds, as he walked them to Janice's old beater of a car. Gently, he tucked the kids into the back seat, buckling them into their car seats. To Janice, he said, "Pop the hood, will you?"

As Janice complied, Jerry bent under the hood. "Olivia, bring me two quarts of oil, please, honey?" To Janice, he said, "It's low again. I'll fill it up now and give you an extra quart of oil. But you've got to remember to add oil each time you fill up with gas. Got it?"

"Yeah, I'll remember. I just forgot in all the rush of packing." As Jerry started to speak, she held up her hand. "I know, I know. I get it. You've told me enough times." Looking into the kind face of her neighbor, she altered the tone of her voice. "Jerry, I can't thank you enough. You and Olivia have been so good to us. I'll remember about the oil, I promise. And I'll let you know how we're doing."

With the kids settled in the back seat amid snacks and toys, Janice headed out on I-15 north. It was five hours until they'd get to Las Vegas where she hoped to find a cheap place for them to spend the night, preferably not in the car. She'd planned to get farther than Vegas the first day, but they got a late start. Packing up with two little boys underfoot took more time than she'd anticipated.

But here they were, on their way to a new life. A better life.

She'd miss Olivia and Jerry. They'd been such a help with the boys, always willing to babysit when she had to work shifts at the diner. Well, those times weren't always due to work; sometimes she needed a night out with Luke.

Now, though, they'd be a family, a true family with a mother and a father. Luke would be fine with the boys once he met them. He had to be.

Squawks from the back seat. Matt. For a kid who couldn't talk, he certainly made his feelings known.

"Mom." Alex, ever watchful of his little brother, kicked the back of the driver's seat. "Mom, Matt needs you."

"I can't look now. I'm driving. Can't you help him?"

"He stinks. He pooped."

Oh, good grief. The odor reached the front seat now. Could she ignore it?

Less than 10 miles down the road, Alex kicked Janice's seat again. "Mooom. He *really* stinks. And he's mushing it all around."

True, too true. No one could mess a diaper like Mateo. Matt, she corrected herself. While in the US, they used the anglicized forms of their names, rather than their given names. Matt, not Mateo. Janice, not Juana. It's just that being on the road felt like they should be going back home to Rosarito. With a sigh, Janice pulled over to the side of the road.

This had to be her least favorite job in the world. When she'd dreamed of having a baby of her own, *this* had not entered her thoughts.

Pulling her youngest from his car seat, holding him with extended arms, Janice draped Matt on top of her car's trunk. Luckily the temperature was moderate today, so the metal wasn't blisteringly hot. She'd hate to mess up one of their few towels by laying it under him.

Matt squirmed. "No! Hold still." Serve the kid right if he fell off the car. It was his fault they had to stop to deal with this mess.

Geez, the boy was almost three. Would this go on forever?

Matt hated getting his diaper changed. How come? Did he like wallowing in his messes? *She* certainly didn't enjoy this.

Why couldn't he have a normal crap like everyone else? In the toilet, or at least as a solid ball in his diaper. Yeah, that was normal, wasn't it? Not this vile, reeking goo that oozed out every possible crack around his diaper, no matter how tightly she taped the thing onto him.

Janice turned her head away, trying not to gag. She pulled her t-shirt up over her nose, but it gave her little protection against the disgusting stench.

The kid ate the same things as the rest of them. How could he turn it into such a godawful mess? Alex hadn't done this since he was a tiny baby, and certainly not once he was on solid food.

Kicking his legs in the air, Matt grinned up at his mom, those shiny, white front teeth glistening as drool rolled down his cheek. Her heart softened, just a little. He was a cute little devil, took after his father, wherever he was.

That had been a fun few months when she hooked up with that guy in Rosarito, south of the border. She was there introducing 18-month-old Alejandro to his grand-mother, Elena. Luckily, the old lady was so thrilled to meet her grandson that she had no problem looking after him while Janice took a much-needed break. Single parenting a toddler was a lot of work, especially when there was no child support or help from the sperm donor, even if he had provided fun while it lasted.

Juana was young; she deserved some fun. It was nice to just be herself again, Juana, rather than assuming the Americanized name, Janice, and pretending to blend in in California. But you did what you had to do.

The result though was this - Matteo. Now she had two boys to look after, all by herself.

Not for long. Soon, Luke would support them. Her mom had always had men to look after her. So far, that had not worked out for Janice, especially after Matteo's birth.

Matt, she reminded herself, not Matteo. Where they were going, fewer people had Hispanic roots. She needed to stick to their American names.

Shoot! Daydreaming didn't pay, especially during a diaper change with Matt. The child wiggled onto his side. With her elbow, Janice rolled him back into position, then lay her forearm across his stomach to hold him in place, while she tugged the soiled diaper from under his bottom.

Shit! Literally. His squirming and the leaky diaper spread filth onto her sleeve as her arm pressed his abdomen to the car. Yanking her arm back, she examined the splotch. Some mocha mush clung to the fabric.

Warning Matt not to move, she squatted down in the

ditch by the side of the road. Plucking handfuls of dried, parched grass, she attempted to remove some of the foul excrement from her shirt. While the chunks scraped off, she succeeded in spreading the puke-brown stain.

A yell from the car made her look up. Alex, turned around in his seat, pointing out the rear window. "Mom, he's gonna fall!"

Bounding up, Janice caught Matt's left arm as he careened off the side of the car. Quickly wrapping her other hand under his armpit, she hoisted the child back onto the trunk of the car. Just about to lay him down, she noticed the telltale brown streak Matt created as he slid off the car.

Grabbing him none too gently, Janice moved to the other side of the car to try again with a fresh spot.

She got the job done. Not well done but done. The kid needed a bath, but there wasn't so much as a puddle around here. If she was home, she'd throw him in the tub and let the water do the job for her. Once when she'd left him playing in the bathtub, she'd returned to find him drinking his bath water, with suspicious brown bits floating all around him. Kids.

For now, she was stuck with diapers and wipes. Wipes were expensive. Didn't the kid realize that? At this rate, they'd run out before they got to Luke's place. The town of Embarrass, Minnesota was a long way away, and she only had so much money to get them through this trip.

Chapter Two

Janice

Leaving all the windows down for the next half hour helped air out the car's interior. Still the aroma of crap lingered. Old crap. Unhealthy crap, worse than the stench of an unkept, public latrine.

But they were used to it, sort of. It was a fact of life with a kid like Matt. Surely, he'd grow out of this phase soon, and be out of diapers.

It was only one of many things she wished he'd grow out of, albeit this topped the list. As he got older, Alex became easier to look after, more independent, more compliant, seeming to know that he should not make his mother's life any more difficult than it already was. He was a good boy. Matt, on the other hand, didn't seem to get it. There were many things he did not seem to get.

Janice was not the kind of mother to keep baby books, those cutesy pink or blue things where doting parents wrote down notes about when their kid gave a smile unrelated to gas, tried smashed peas, took his first step, said his first word, and stopped needing a diaper. Nope, a single mom, struggling to keep food on the table, didn't have time for such indulgences.

But she didn't remember toilet training Alex being such a big deal. It just sort of happened. Well, maybe Olivia and Jerry had something to do with that, but why didn't they try with Matt as well?

And Janice was absolutely positive that by this age, Alex was talking. He was most certainly walking. Running was more like it.

But three months shy of his third birthday, Matt did none of these things.

The desert landscape had never been her thing. Although her hometown of Rosarito was arid, there was the nearby ocean. San Diego was more than just shades of brown as well.

Dotting the highway, small towns appeared, then disappeared in her rearview mirror. They got in the way when the highway wound right through them, causing traffic to slow to a crawl.

Don't complain. She could hear Olivia's voice in her ear. See this as an opportunity. She was moving to a small town to be with Luke, so maybe she should learn to appreciate the treasures towns offered.

Like that. An ancient Victorian, three-storey house stood out, a painted lady amid drab browns. Exotic with vibrant purple shutters alongside each window, wraparound porches with swings and rocking chairs. Sanctum. What a name for a bed and breakfast. A sanctuary. If she was by herself, she'd be tempted to stop at such a place. But no, she needed to keep going, get to Luke and the life they had planned together. There she'd find her own sanctum, a place of her own. Smiling, she sped up and continued her journey.

Pulling over, Janice scrolled through the travel guidebook Olivia gave her, searching for a Vegas hotel room that would fit her budget. The first ten minutes were discouraging. She shouldn't have to choose between giving them a place to sleep and eating, should she?

"Quit it!" She hollered at Alex, whose little feet thumped away at the back of her seat. "I'm trying to find us a hotel room."

"But Mom, Matt and me are hungry."

"Aren't we all?"

The kid didn't let up, almost drowning out Matt's howls. Kids. Opening her door, Janice left the car. Nope, she still couldn't hear herself think about the racket her sons made. Back in the driver's seat, she pressed the buttons to raise all the windows, then turned off the ignition.

There. Now it was quieter out here. The boys weren't silent by any means, but muffled, so she could concentrate. It would get hot in the car, yeah, but if she could just concentrate, she'd have this figured out quickly and turn the air conditioning back on as they got on their way.

What? Had she missed something? Quickly she flipped back, and yes, there it was. Something in the 30s. Yes! That was the price range she could handle. But wait. Were there resort fees? Those things could double the price for the room.

She read aloud:

RIO Las Vegas Hotel Suites

Our over 500 sq. ft. Luxury Masquerade Suites feature two queen beds with floor-to-ceiling windows offering spectacular sunset views of Las Vegas's Spring Mountains. Amenities include mini-refrigerator, sofa, flat screen TV with On Demand movies, in-room safe, iron/board and hair dryer.

Rates From ~~$36~~ $32

And would you look at that picture? Wow! Even if the photo was taken a decade ago, it was still nicer than anything she'd ever stayed in before. And the size - it was almost as big as her whole apartment had been. Two beds, so she wouldn't have to put up with getting kicked by restless, sleeping little boys all night. The hair dryer meant that she could wash the shirt she wore and make sure it was dried enough to wear tomorrow. She raised her arm toward her face and took a sniff. Yep. It was not just the nasty brown stain that offended her. Maybe she could wash the back of Matt's shirt as well where some of the noxious excrement had seeped onto it.

No resort fees. Free parking. Restaurants on site. That meant she didn't have to drag two kids through the teeming streets of Vegas to feed them. Matt was so heavy to carry far. When would that kid learn to walk?

Janice pulled off at the next exit, found a phone booth, and rang the hotel. It would be just her luck to have this amazing room all sold out before she could get there. But no, she was in luck for once in her miserable life. Maybe things were truly turning around. She was on her way to a new life with a great guy who would look after her, plus she had an amazing room in which to spend the night. It was an omen of better things to come.

Luke

It was cold. Colder than anything he'd experienced in his life. Colder than any human could be expected to survive. Did people actually *choose* to live in places like this? And they told him winter had barely begun here in Embarrass, Minnesota, one of the coldest places in the continental USA.

The sensations created by the arctic air started with just a tingling at the ends of his fingers, then sank deeper into his sinews and tendons until they ignited in a bizarre combination of blazing fire and numbing ice at the same time.

Removing his right glove, Luke blew on his hand, flexing his fingers to get some life back into his frozen digits. Maybe not frozen. The guys told him that when something froze you couldn't feel it any longer. Nope, the pain in his fingers meant his hand was not frozen, just damned cold.

Cursing, he put the glove back on, tightening the Velcro closure at the wrist. He'd learned not to let cold air leak between his sleeve and the decent work gloves provided by the company. Thank God for this one perk. His own gloves had holes in them, and he had to double the fabric over when he clung to the steering wheel of the old beater of a truck his grandmother left him.

Things got tough in San Diego. It wasn't so bad until he lost his job. Not his fault that the company folded. Times were hard and lots of businesses struggled. That didn't mean *he* had to, did it? Yeah, apparently it did. There were no jobs to be found and his meagre savings dwindled faster than the under-counter kegs at his fave drinking hole.

Then came the news that he'd inherited his grandmother's house. He hardly knew her, just some vague memories of playing at her place as a boy.

Those were good times. Back then his dad and mom got along. Visiting Gran was great - a road trip, staying at hotels, eating in restaurants, then running free through the fields surrounding her tiny farmhouse.

Life changed, though, as it's wont to do. Sucks, but what can you do? Dad lost his job in the oil patch, and things got harder around home, leaner. The old man never found a job to adequately replace that salary. Mom's work at the cleaners kept food on the table, mostly. Food and booze, in varying proportions, depending on the mood in the household at any given time.

Luke was not a big man and that was on his parents' shoulders. They'd rather drink than fill their son's belly with the food he needed to reach his potential.

Now he was taxed to keep up with his workmates. The heavy branches some hauled with ease required supreme effort from Luke. He hated that he grunted under their weight, but sometimes he couldn't control it. That's the extent of the bellyaching he allowed himself.

At first, working for a tree trimming company seemed great. Breezes from the lake moderated the August temperatures. For a guy who hated being cooped up, this was the ideal job. Decent people to work with, an okay wage, and a boss who promised to give him as many hours as he could.

Pity that he had to work at all, but such was life. He'd hoped that inheriting a house had meant a little money with it as well.

Nope. Yeah, he got the land and house all right, such as it was.

The place in his memories twenty some years past was small, but quaint. Space to run, to ride the rickety bike stored in an old shed that listed to one side. That shed was cool; when he pushed on its side with all his might, he could make the building creak and sway. His mom ordered him to never go in there, but the place was full of treasures, including the bike.

Well, now that building was a heap of twisted and splintered timbers on the ground. Not even rats found it habitable these days. Maybe there were a few treasures buried in the rubble, maybe one day he'd poke around.

For now, he needed to make a living. Sure, there was no rent to pay, but he still had to eat. And, as winter approached, the house leaked frigid air. Yesterday when he woke up, the glass of water beside his bed had a skiff of ice on top. Heating the place was going to be a bummer for sure this winter.

While his boss was flush with tree trimming contracts in the summer and fall, they'd slowed to a trickle now. The only times Luke got called to come work recently was when tree branches went down in a storm. Like now. Perched in the truck's damned utility bucket, high above the ground, arms extended to run a chainsaw that weighed more than the boulders lining the walk to his front door, freezing off parts of his anatomy he'd rather keep.

Don't think about it. Just get the job done and get down from this perch.

He'd never met his grandfather. Word had it, he used to farm the land around the house. Some grain, some hay, some animals. Something to think about, maybe a way to make some good cash. How hard could it be?

Soon Janice would be here. She'd find work easily; women could always do stuff in towns like this. Stores, two diners, cleaning houses, there was plenty of work for her. Her income would see them through the lean times when he didn't get many shifts.

Chapter Three

Unbelievable! The most beautiful place she'd ever seen. Who'd have thought that one day she'd stay in digs like this? Yes, things were looking up.

Twirling slowly in place, Janice took it all in. Floor-to-ceiling windows filled one wall. In the distance were Las Vegas' Spring Mountains. Below, the city spread out in all its glory. Soon night would fall, bringing a panorama of twinkling lights. She filled her lungs. Even the air in the room smelled fresh. No mold. No rust. No rotting food in a trash can.

Peeking into the bathroom, she saw nothing but sparkling white fixtures and fluffy, folded towels. Not one of them on the floor, not a thing out of place.

Back in the main room, Alex squealed in delight, jumping on the queen-sized bed. Matt managed to climb up but lacked the balance to mimic his brother. Instead, he sat as close as he could to Alex's jumping feet, shrieking with glee as each bounce knocked him over.

To the side of the room were two easy chairs, plusher

than any she'd ever hoped to own. The deep, dark brown carpet surrounded and comforted her tired feet. Near the seating area a large TV commanded attention.

Not bad, not bad at all. Maybe they should stay here two nights.

Sinking into one of the comfy chairs, she switched on the TV, put her feet on the matching ottoman, and ignored her sons.

It worked for a while, but not nearly long enough.

Matt started his mewling noises. He didn't have a wide range of verbal communication strategies. This particular noise could mean two things - either he needed something put into his mouth, or he'd evacuated something from the other end. In, out, in, out. It never ended.

Her nose gave the air a sniff. Nope, nothing wafted this way yet.

"Mom, we're hungry."

Ah, Alex interpreted his brother's complaint and echoed it.

"In a bit." She put her head back down against the chair back and pointed the remote at the giant TV. She'd give herself another five minutes of relaxation. That wasn't too much to ask, was it?

Apparently.

The bouncing stopped and the boys left the bed to drape themselves over their mother.

Peace was over. From experience, when her sons got *hangry*, things went from bad to worse.

Pulling open the desk drawer, she inspected the options at the Rio. No sense going somewhere in the car then needing to find a parking spot again. And she certainly wasn't walking the Strip with her kids when she had to carry Matt.

The cheapest option looked like Smashburger. Something a kid would eat and how bad could their prices be for a burger?

At least service was prompt and there weren't many people in the restaurant. But, that much for a burger? For a kid? By the time she bought them hamburgers, fries, and sodas, their steal-of-a-deal hotel room didn't look quite such a bargain. She picked fries from the boys' plates, knowing they'd be unable to finish some of their meals, especially Matt. She'd eat whatever they left. In the meantime, she splurged on a beer for herself, something local they had on tap. It was okay, but she'd have preferred a Bud.

Back in the room, she stuck the boys in the bathtub, marveling at how clean it was. How did you even get porcelain that shiny?

Knowing they'd amuse themselves for a good half hour, she tucked her feet under her and settled into the soft chair cushions to flick through the channels on the TV. Hmm. Disappointingly similar to the channels she got at home.

Still, it was lovely just being here. The hotel had generously stocked the minibar for her. She emptied the contents, lining up tiny bottles of vodka, rum, and bourbon for later, and the chocolate bars and bags of chips as bedtime treats for the boys. On second thought, she hid the bars and chips in a drawer. They'd do for breakfast, saving her money tomorrow.

The boys' sounds were muted through the closed bathroom door. Inky blackness enveloped the floor-to-ceiling windows, with lights twinkling in the darkness, illuminating the never still Strip. Tempting to stay here in this room, pretend this was her life, even for just a few days.

She sipped on her beer from the mini bar and considered. No, with food this expensive, they couldn't afford to spend a second night in Vegas. Pity.

Chapter Four

Janice studied the map in the guidebook. If she took I-15 N, they should be able to make it straight through Utah and up into Wyoming today. A longer driving day than yesterday. Two big pushes, with overnights in Wyoming, then in North Dakota, and one final long driving day, then they'd be there. Home. Their new home, a quaint farmhouse with space for the boys to roam and play.

She'd wisely hid the pop, chips, and chocolate bars in a bag. Sure enough, when the boys became restless and cranky from being trapped in their car seats for so long, doling out the treats a bit at a time kept them quiet and occupied. At least, for a while. Now they started up again, Alex saying he needed to pee.

Glancing at her dashboard gauges, Janice saw that if she didn't stop soon, her car would also protest. The gas indicator was nearing the far left. It wasn't like gas stations were every few miles in these rural areas. She could hear Jerry's words in her head. "You keep that gas tank topped up, you hear? You don't want to run out of gas and be stranded somewhere. You're heading north; it gets cold up there, and you'd be mighty chilly sleeping in the car. Might even die." Okay, she got it. Even his final admonition about putting oil in whenever she filled up with gas. The man was a worry wort. She watched for signs for the next town. They'd left Vegas less than four hours ago, and still had a long way to go today.

There. The exit for Beaver, Utah was in two miles. Signs along the highway advertised the skiing on Beaver Mountain. Wonder what that would be like? Spending all her life within a few hundred miles of the Mexico/US western border, she'd never seen snow. Yet. Luke promised she'd get to experience snow this year in Embarrass, Minnesota. That'd be exciting.

A cool thing about small towns was service. A kid came out to pump her gas. Nice. No need to get her hands dirty, and she let the boys stretch their legs while someone else filled her car.

Good time for a potty break. Following Olivia's advice, she dutifully sat Matt on the toilet, holding him in position long enough for something to happen. It didn't. It never did. Sighing, she refastened his diaper. How had this worked with Alex? One minute he'd been sitting on a potty chair to do his business, the next thing she knew, he was standing to pee, and wiping his own bum. Why couldn't it be that easy with Matt?

Propping Matt between her right hip and the sink, Janice washed her son's hands, then his face. There was little she could do about the melted chocolate smeared into his shirt.

Hoisting Matt to a better position at her waist, she led

the boys from the washroom to the cash register near the front of the store. The aisles were landmines of temptation, all sorts of treats at the eye levels of two small boys.

"Mom, we're hungry." Predictably, the complaint came from Alex, the spokesman for his brother. They'd already consumed a bag of chips each, plus a candy bar. Man, those kids could eat.

Now was as good a time as any to buy something for lunch. But not here, not something from this aisle. She led them to the glass doors of the dairy section. Milk was what the kids should have.

Oh, but look at the prices. She'd save some money by buying the gallon size, but it might go off before they finished it. And how would the kids handle drinking from that big jug in the car? The smallest cartons of milk were pricey, and there was no way of closing them once opened.

Janice returned to the soda pop aisle, pondering her choices as Alex whined. She grabbed a six pack of mini tins. The kids usually downed one of those at a sitting. Still, just how much pop should a boy consume? She glanced back at the milk area, weighing her options.

A woman nearby noticed. Turning up one side of her mouth, she sympathized. "Ya gotta do what ya gotta do, whether you feel like it or not. Right?"

Janice nodded. Once they were settled with Luke, she'd pay more attention to nutrition. Right now, she needed to do what she needed to do to get them there.

"Cute kids," the woman commented. Sharing a smile, the lady batted at a wasp flying by her. Her hand knocked the insect off its trajectory, landing on the side of Matt's nose. The vengeful critter sank in its stinger.

It took a second or two, then Matt screamed. And

screamed and screamed, his hands sheltering his injured nose.

Pulling the child's hands from his face, Janice peered at the damage. Already the nose was swelling.

"Quick, get him next door." The woman ordered. "There's a pharmacy near the back. Someone there will know what to do." She started toward the door. "Come, I'll show you. Maybe the kid's allergic to bee stings."

Janice ran after her, the sobbing boy in her arms.

Alex grabbed onto the edge of her shirt and ran with them. "Is he okay? Mom, is Matt gonna be okay?"

The pharmacist heard them coming. Everyone in the store did. He left his spot behind the counter to meet them.

The woman held Matt's hands so the pharmacist could get a look at the rapidly swelling nose.

"Ah, the stinger's still in there. Come this way." He led them into an office with two chairs. "Hold him as still as you can."

Taking a seat, Janice gripped Matt's legs between her thighs, wrapping her arms around his chest. The woman placed one hand under the boy's chin and the other on top of his head, trying to keep him steady. The pharmacist pressed Matt's forehead to his mom's chest, shielding the child's eyes, and wielded tweezers with his right hand.

"There." The man held the tiny, offensive stinger in the air. "Got it." He dabbed some cooling antibiotic gel onto the spot. "He'd better have some Benadryl to dampen any reaction to the sting. Has he had it before? Does he have allergies?"

Janice shook her head.

He caught her wary look and understood. "I have some

free sample boxes here." Under his direction, Janice encouraged Matt to swallow a teaspoonful of the Children's Benadryl. "I need to warn you. It will make him sleepy."

Janice gave a weak smile. "That's probably good. We have a long drive ahead of us."

The pharmacist handed her two more sample boxes of the medicine. "You might want to give him some more every four to six hours until the swelling goes down and he doesn't seem as bothered by the sting. But no more than 6 doses in 24 hours." Pulling several tissues from a box on his desk, he handed them to Janice.

She tried to clean some of the snot from her son's face, then hoisted him to her hip. "Thank you so much for your help, sir."

Eyeing her and the boys, the man opened a cupboard on the wall. "Do you have any antibiotic cream with you?" He held out a small cardboard box. "Not a bad idea to keep some with you when you have boys. Never know when you'll need it. And this young fellow here might be rubbing at that sting. Don't want to get it infected, so use this."

Retracing her steps back to the gas station, Janice paid for her gas. Alex, ever mindful of his stomach, reminded her that he was hungry, so she let him choose the snacks he wanted, adding a six-pack of soda to their stash, and a bag of Doritos for herself. Glancing around, she made sure she had everything. Yep, two kids, drinks, snack foods, gas. Got it.

Chapter Five

It worked. Just like the pharmacist said, the Benadryl made Matt sleepy. He was out before he'd barely finished half of his bag of chips. Alex snagged the bag before it fell from his brother's limp fingers and finished it off.

That meant both boys were quiet, at least for a while, so Janice pushed on. Make hay while the sun shines. Tee hee. Getting into this rural lingo already.

Three hours later, she needed a potty break, as did Alex. Pulling into a rest stop, Janice debated what to do. Leave Matt here alone while they went inside, or wake him up and take him with them? Matt wasn't bad when he woke on his own but waking him before he was ready created one grisly child.

"Mom, I really need to go!"

Alex's reminder made her decision for her. It would take too long to rouse Matt, get him out of the car seat and carry him inside. They'd only be a few minutes.

And that's all it took. They were back, and Matt hadn't even stirred. Good thing, too, because Janice realized she'd forgotten to lock the car doors. There was no one else around, so it was safe. Even if he had awakened, and undid his belt on his own, how fast could he crawl away?

Back on the road, Janice checked her map, glancing up occasionally to make sure she remained in her lane. Good thing there was little traffic on these highways. She needed to keep an eye on things. At Salt Lake City, she'd turned onto highway 80, but would need to take an exit to head north. Not for a while yet, though.

Thump, thump on the back of her seat. She pressed her lips in annoyance. Alex's way of letting her know he was getting tired of this. Well, she was, too. He'd just have to be patient. She handed back what remained of her bag of Doritos. That would keep him quiet for a while.

They drove for almost another hour before there was any noise from the back seat. Then Matt woke up. "Hi, sweetie," Janice said over her shoulder. "How are you feeling?"

Shoot! That reminded him. The little boy put his hand to his nose, whimpering. The whimpers turned into moans, then growls. There was no other word to explain it.

"Sh. Alex is sleeping. You can't wake him up."

Too late.

Now both little boys howled. It was all Janice could do to not join in. Okay, okay. Deep breaths, that's what Olivia said to do when the kids drove her nuts. Try to calm yourself before you say or do anything. Right. Like *Olivia'd* ever driven halfway across the country with two kids like this.

But it wouldn't take much to make the situation worse, and there was no Olivia or Jerry around to rescue her. It was up to Janice, and Janice alone.

If she had any hope of improving their lives, she needed to get her family to Embarrass, Minnesota, where Luke waited for them. Well, for her, but that was a small detail they'd work around when the time came. For now, she needed to put miles on this car.

Pulling over at a rest area with picnic tables, swings, and what looked like washrooms, Janice shut off the car. Maybe letting the boys play for a few minutes would help. They'd been cooped up for two days now, and so had she, the luxury of their Vegas hotel stay a distant memory. "Wanna swing?"

Alex fumbled with his seat belt in response. She helped, then let him go. She wiped Matt's dripping nose with the edge of his t-shirt, lifted him from the car seat, and carried him to the swings. Thank goodness there was a baby swing, the type where she could strap him in. His balance was not good enough for regular swings, although she hoped it soon would. It would not be long before she'd be unable to sandwich his growing body into these swings meant for younger kids.

This was one of the times Janice wished she still smoked. The scene just called for a smoke break. But it was a costly habit, one she had let go.

Fifteen minutes. That's all they could spare before hitting the road again.

The kids calmed down. *She* calmed down. Yes, stopping had been the right thing to do. "Okay, guys, let's get going." The expected whines were not as vocal as she'd anticipated.

Strapped back in their seats, they headed onto the highway. They'd barely gone twenty miles before the kids were fussing. Again.

Janice blew out a breath. This was not going to work. She needed to concentrate on where they were going. That incessant kicking on the back of her seat got on her nerves, as did the non-stop grousing.

Pulling over, she dug out her secret weapon - two containers of Tootsie Roll logs, the boys' favorite treats. Gooey, yeah. Sugary, yeah. Nutritious, nah, but they'd keep them quiet for a while. Taking them out of her purse, she spied something else, something that didn't used to be there. Benadryl.

Reaching into the back seat, she gave each boy a candy log; their whining stopped immediately. She had some peace in which to read the label on the Benadryl. The stuff had put Matt to sleep quite quickly. Would it work on Alex as well?

What was she thinking? Giving her kids medicine when they didn't need it? The pharmacist implied there was a good chance that Matt actually *did* need it. Not Alex, though. But would it hurt him?

It was for their collective good to get to Minnesota and their new life as quickly as possible. If the boys were quiet, she could drive much longer, probably into the night even. She looked at the bottle, then at her boys, their sticky hands and faces covered in brown sugary stuff. Should I?

The words of the woman at the gas station echoed in her mind. "You do what you gotta do…". Wise woman. Janice climbed out of the car and reached into the back seat.

Chapter Six

Peace reigned in the car. Almost too much peace. As the hours wore on and they ate up the miles, Janice became sleepy, too. She turned on the radio, dialing in a country station. Singing along would help keep her awake.

Finally. A sign up ahead announced the approach of Rawlins, Wyoming. Pressing the dome light in the ceiling, Janice checked her map. Yep, that was the place where she'd need to get off this major highway and onto to the smaller 220 road to take her to Casper, then farther north.

They'd made good time today, excellent time, in fact. But now she needed some rest if she was going to get up and do this again tomorrow.

There was a Super 8 just off Interstate 80. Ah, its vacancy sign was on. Making sure to lock the boys securely in the car, she entered the lobby to get their room.

Hmph. It cost far more than their gorgeous Vegas room, but hey, what could you do? She'd saved some cash on meals today since the boys slept through supper, making the money Luke'd sent her go just a little further.

First, she carried in their suitcases and turned down the bed the boys would share. Then she went back for Alex. The child didn't stir as she carried him into the ground-floor room, removed his shoes and pants and put him on the bed. Next, she reached in the other side of the car's back seat for Matt, pulling him into her arms.

Yuk! He was wet, soaked right through his diaper and pants. His car seat looked damp, but it would dry by morning.

If she tried to change his diaper now, it would wake him up, and he'd never settle back down. Surely, his racket would wake his brother, so she'd never get the sleep she needed. No, his diaper would have to wait until morning. She'd deal with things then.

She plunked herself on the other bed repeating her new mantra the last thing she thought of. You do what you gotta do….

The boys awoke cranky and far earlier than their mother had hoped for. It was done now, and time to get back on the road. At least this motel came with a free continental breakfast.

Washing their hands and faces, the reek of stale urine almost overpowered Janice. A quick scrub with the wash-cloth would not be enough. She poured a bath, a sure-fire way to get the crank out of her boys' voices. Playing in the water was one of their favorite things.

Except this tub didn't look like the one at the Rio in Vegas. Years and years of scrubbing had worn the shiny surface from the beige porcelain, making it no longer look like a matching set with the toilet and sink, although the sink's lack of luster was closing in on that of its larger partner. Didn't matter. It would soak the grime off Matt's body.

What to do about his clothes, though? He didn't have that many shirts or pants that she could follow her instinct and chuck them. Nor did she want to waste her precious cash reserves on unnecessary purchases. She opted for scrubbing them in the sink. If she put them on the back window ledge of the car, they should dry eventually.

Scrubbed and happier, she carried their suitcase to the trunk of the car. With Alex trailing behind, Janice carried Matt to the small area that held a few tables and a counter full of breakfast choices. Filling bowls, she brought her sons dry cereal, then returned with milk, spoons, and sugar for them. While they stuffed their mouths, she brought three glasses or orange juice to the table, started a bagel toasting, and got herself a cup of coffee.

Ah, quiet. She had a minute to look around. No other travellers joined them in the breakfast area, thankfully. Her eye spied a Belgian waffle machine, the kind they'd used in the diner where she worked back home. A treat. The boys would love it, and it would keep them quiet for a while longer.

Cutting up their waffles for them, a thought occurred. Why not make a couple more and to take with them in the car? The boys could eat them with their hands - lunch solved. More inspection turned up lids for the styrofoam cups, so she filled three with juice, pushing the lids on securely. She wrapped the extra waffles in napkins, hiding them in her purse. Next, she spread out napkins, pouring drying cereal into the center of each, then trying the ends in a knot. Voila! Snacks for the boys. Since the kids were occupied with their food, and no one else was around, Janice took her now-bulging handbag out to the car where she unloaded her treasures.

Maybe she'd look for another Super 8 for tonight if they were all like this.

In the parking lot, Janice studied the map. This next bit was tricky. Got it. She knew the route. They'd head toward South Dakota, then travel north, until they reached North Dakota. Hopefully they'd make it that far before stopping for the night. Yes, she was confident they would, now that she had her secret weapon, and the boys would sleep, leaving her alone to drive.

Pulling onto the highway, something on the dashboard caught her eye. A red light was on. Pretty sure that wasn't there yesterday, although she'd been tired, focusing her bleary eyes on the road, not the interior of the car.

Nothing to worry about. This was an old car. Warning lights came on all the time, and it was never anything important. Jerry took care of things for her. She had a twinge of regret that he and Olivia were no longer in her life.

Chapter Seven

Okay. From Rawlins, she needed to find I-90 north. Got it.

They stopped in Spearfish, South Dakota for a potty break. They all needed one. The snacks had helped keep the boys occupied during the five-hour drive, but they weren't the only ones restless.

Dairy Queen worked, less messy than Taco Bell food for kids, or so Janice though. Turns out ice cream drips trump burrito drippings any day. Next time she'd know better. Good thing her "next times" were winding down. They were over halfway to their destination, and their new life.

Could she do another seven hours and push through to Fargo, North Dakota? Janice used her rearview mirror to glance in the back. Fresh diaper on Matt, their bladders empty and bellies full, they seemed content. But it had already been almost five hours of traveling. Another seven was pretty extreme for active little boys. For her too. But it would put them that much closer to home.

Home. A cozy farmhouse with some land around it. No noisy, or nosey neighbors. No worrying about the kids running out in front of traffic. No worries about getting mugged walking home from the bus stop after a late shift at work.

Maybe they could get a dog. Yeah, dogs were good for kids. She'd always wanted a dog when she was a little girl, one that would sleep at her feet and jump with joy to see her. Surely Luke would like that, too.

The idyllic images in her mind spurred her on. "Kids, want a Tootsie Roll?"

Immediate responses, all positive.

"Okay, but you need to drink this first." Bless that pharmacist. The swelling on Matt's nose was hardly noticeable now.

She sipped her fourth energy drink of day. Pricey things, but they worked, especially with an added 5-Hour Energy Shot.

Somewhere between Dickinson and Bismarck, North Dakota, the car made a funny noise. At first it was faint over the tunes blasting from the radio. The kids slept like the dead, but Janice needed something to keep her going. After all, she needed her head in the game if she was to keep driving.

The growl stopped. Maybe she imagined it. Maybe it was just some weird bass thing with the music.

There. Up ahead. The sign for Bismarck. Good. Her bladder was bursting and the buzz from the final energy drink had worn off. She needed to pee and get a new drink. A glance at the fuel gauge told her she also needed gas.

That growling noise was back. She turned off the radio

this time to be sure, but yeah, she'd heard it even over the ranting on the News Talk Radio station.

She knew what Jerry would say - "Check the oil, babe. Don't forget."

Well, she wouldn't. This time. Sheesh. Who could remember every single time, and who could afford it?

Pulling into the station, Janice was thankful that the boys didn't even stir in their car seats. As she pumped the gas into the car, she could see their little faces in the reflection from the station's flood lights.

They were pretty cute, especially in their sleep. Luke wouldn't be able to resist them. If he wasn't used to kids, well, mostly they were good boys, even if Matt had his problems. Just a bit delayed; he'd catch up soon. Didn't all kids develop at their own pace? She'd read that somewhere. Yeah, Luke would like them.

And for those times when they got too rambunctious, well, she had a secret weapon now. One full bottle left, and surely Luke would buy them more for when they needed it. Too bad no one had told her about this wonder drug years ago. Live and learn, they say.

After hanging up the nozzle and screwing the gas cap back on, Janice popped the lid of the hood. Jerry'd been adamant that she know how to do these things. Not that she much liked checking the oil, but Jerry ragged on her until she could do it. Problem was, the engine was far from pristine, and she hated getting grease on her fingers, or even worse, some of that grunge under her nails.

Pulling on the dipstick's plastic handle, Janice used an old piece of tissue from her pocket to wipe it clean. Bits of stuff clung to the rod's surface, kind of like crumbs or filings. Hmm. She didn't remember that before, just semi-clean oily stuff. Nothing gritty, or as dark as this. Oh, well, maybe she just didn't remember correctly. Jerry mostly did this for her. Too bad this station was self-serve with no attendant to do the dirty job for her.

Something wasn't right. She reinserted the dipstick, more carefully this time, and withdrew it again. Still the same. Nothing. There was no glistening oil line in between the empty and full markings as there usually was. She repeated the procedure again. And a fourth time.

Was there no oil? No, that couldn't be right. Jerry had filled it before she left San Diego, even given her a spare quart to bring along. His words echoed in her head, admonishing her to put in oil every time she got gas.

Well, sheesh. She had a lot on her mind, a lot of responsibility getting herself and these kids half-way across the country. Who could blame her for forgetting one itty bitty thing?

Hoping to avoid having to put out more money, she used the quart of oil Jerry'd put in the trunk, draining every last drop. She waited a minute, then checked the dipstick again. Nothing. Maybe it hadn't had enough time to run down yet. She'd just go use the restroom, then come back and check again.

Five minutes later, the dipstick remained free of any signs of oil. Janice bought another quart and added it, then went inside to pay for her purchases.

Another check. Still, the dipstick didn't register any oil. It must be a faulty stick. She'd just already added two quarts.

Slamming shut the hood, and turning the key in the ignition, she got back on the highway.

Three hours, then they'd be in Fargo.

The growling was back, but louder now. Not even the radio at full volume drowned it out.

Was it really a growling? Jerry always asked her to listen closely so she could describe the kind of noise her old beater made, and where it came from. Not easy to do either of those things.

Now, though, Janice thought she'd tell Jerry it was more of a grinding, than a growl, maybe like metal on metal. What could cause that?

Maybe in Fargo she could find a mechanic willing to look at it cheap. How much could it cost to get someone to just have a look? Well, nothing to do for now but carry on.

Valley City was in her rearview mirror. Less than an hour to go until Fargo. For a little while, her anxiety settled down as the car's grinding reverted to its former growls. Maybe that oil she'd put in finally circulated.

She shook her head to keep alert. This driving was tough. If she wasn't so determined to get them to Luke, she'd have given in and taken a room back in Bismarck.

Luke said he liked a person who was goal oriented. Well, that fit Janice just fine. She had a goal of reaching Luke, the man who would look after them for the rest of their lives.

Chapter Eight

Was it her imagination?

No, the noise was louder, almost drowning out the Luke Combs song on the radio. No longer intermittent, but steady, increasingly loud.

This can't be good. Turning on her signal light, Janice pulled over onto the shoulder. It was too dark to see if there was a proper pull off spot up ahead. So, she crept along on the side of the road.

With an ear-splitting grind, the motor stopped. Just stopped dead.

Loosening her clenched grip on the steering wheel, Janice took in a deep breath. Then another. Olivia told her to do that three times before doing anything. Three wasn't enough this time.

Glancing to check that the boys were still asleep, Janice thanked the pharmacy gods for meds. She had enough to deal with right now without adding two howling boys to the mix.

With her right hand, she switched off the ignition, and put the car into park. Counting the seconds out loud, she waited a full minute, then gave it an extra ten seconds just for good measure before trying to restart the car.

Just a grinding. No reassuring turning over of the moving parts. Try it again. Just a click this time. Maybe if she held the key in the start position, it'd get the idea. No, nothing. It would not go. Stupid car!

Wondering if oil had been the problem, Janice pulled the latch that held down the car's hood. Stepping out of the car, her foot plunged into six inches of white stuff. Snow. Yeah, she'd always wanted to see snow, but not this way.

Where had it come from? The highway was clear, but in the dark, she hadn't been able to see the ditches for the last several hours.

Shaking her foot off, she stepped through the chilly stuff to the front of the car. Fetching the flashlight from the glove box where Jerry stashed one for her, she pulled on the dipstick. Ouch! She'd rested her arm on some mechanic part of the car, the metal scorching her arm. What was up with that? Maybe she'd just never noticed before that things got hot under the hood.

Geez, it was cold out here. That stupid hoodie did nothing to shield her from the wind, that wind blowing ice pellets on her back. She had a fleece jacket in her suitcase, would need to get that out. But even that might not protect her from this biting cold.

The jackets that were fine for the boys on San Diego's winter evenings, would not do here. Luke would have to buy them winter outfits.

They weren't even into Minnesota yet. How much colder could it get?

Not sure what to do next, Janice pulled the hood over her head, and thought about the things she'd seen Jerry do when her car wouldn't start. He sort of jiggled things, played with wires. Well, there weren't that many wires. She gave each one she could reach a wiggle, carefully avoiding the blistering hot metal. At least the wind would cool it off. She jiggled two thick things she thought might be battery cables. There. That oughta do something.

Getting back behind the wheel, she turned the key in the ignition. No reassuring start-up sounds.

She rested her head on the steering wheel. Now what?

While she'd poked under the hood, she'd left her car door open. In a normal life, that shouldn't matter. Now, the interior of the car was cold. Not just a bit chilly, but *cold*. Since she couldn't turn the car on, there was no way to make the heater work.

Shuffling in the back seat caught her attention. The boys were still asleep, but both were moving around in their sleep, no longer peaceful they way they had been for the past hours. Were they getting cold?

Were they going to freeze out here? Was that even a thing? Did people actually die from the cold?

No. Not in America. Maybe way off in the Arctic, but not here. Couldn't happen.

But she was colder than she'd ever been before.

Braving the elements one final time, Janice opened the trunk and brought their suitcase inside. Maybe if she piled all their clothes around them, they'd stay warm enough.

Janice put on all the socks she owned, then removed her sons' shoes and added extra layers of socks. They each only had two pair, but it was better than nothing. She wiggled their feet back into their shoes.

The suitcase lay open on the passenger seat. Janice wedged herself into the back seat, in the small space between the two car seats. Reaching over the seat back, she pulled all the clothing from the suitcase into the back, wrapping them around her sons and herself, saving one pair of socks for her hands. Then, draping one arm around each child, she joined them in a troubled slumber.

It was hard to get comfortable with her body shivering. Checking on her boys, Janice was glad that they were out, oblivious to the cold seeping into their bones. She wondered if the Benadryl would work on her or if she should save it for the kids.

Janice dozed on and off, fitfully, struggling to find a way to cuddle up to preserve body warmth. The little boys whimpered in their sleep.

Noise, again strange noises. These ones interrupted her sleep, just when she'd found a way to keep her feet tucked up under her so that they weren't so numb.

"Lady, hey, lady." A fist banged on the side window. Then the driver's side door opened, and some guy looked in.

Still drowsy, Janice was slow to react. She should have known better. Growing up as she had, she knew never to let down her guard. How had she let herself be this vulnerable? From her cramped position in the backseat, she'd never be able to defend herself.

"Lady, you all right? Whatcha doing out here? You could freeze to death in this weather."

Yeah, well, that was exactly what she was trying *not* to

do. Did he think she dressed this way for the sake of beauty?

The man removed his head from the car and called out to someone. "It's some lady. And she's got two little kids with her."

Bending back down to peer at Janice, he asked. "What are you doing out here in the middle of nowhere? Car trouble?"

What could she do? There was no way Luke could get to them that night even if she had a way to let him know they needed help. Her plan had been to wait it out until daylight, then see what happened. It was a goal of sorts. Baby steps.

Another man opened the passenger front door and poked his head in, sizing up Janice and her sons. Reaching over, he turned the keys in the ignition. "Need to get some heat in here." At the grinding noise the car made, the men looked at each other. "Seized." They both nodded.

"Here's what we're going to do," the second man said. "My truck's running and it's warm. We'll transfer the car seats into the back of my cab and strap the kids in."

"But..." Janice began.

"Lady, you won't last the night out here. Maybe there's a chance, a slim chance, that you would but not these little guys."

Without waiting for her permission, he worked on the car seat in a way that showed he'd done this before. Then he left with Matt and his car seat in his arms. The wind blew away Janice's protests.

As she struggled to get her frozen limbs to respond, the other guy freed Alex's seat from the car and stalked off with the first man.

Within minutes, the first guy was back, tossing any loose

clothing he spied into the suitcase, then zipping it shut. His left hand reached for Janice's arm, tugging her out the car door, helping her to stand. With one arm around her, and the other gripping the suitcase, he led her through the blowing, drifting snow to his pickup.

Chapter Nine

The men spoke to one another in low voices. Janice caught only a few words, something about, "...lacking the sense God gave a...", and "...she'll have a bed for...".

The broad-shouldered man in the passenger seat put a CB radio to his mouth and spoke quietly. Then, tossing the radio onto the dashboard, he stuck his hand over the seat back towards Janice. "Stan." He shook her hand, then nodded at the driver. "This is my brother, Greg. Lucky we came along when we did. Where you headed to?"

"Minnesota."

The brothers looked at each other. "I don't think that car is going to get you there."

Bleakness settled into Janice's heart. Now what? She removed the socks from her hands and flexed her fingers. The tips tingled now that feeling returned in the warmth of the truck cab. The sensation was hard to ignore. Good thing the boys were asleep. By the time they woke up, they'd be fine.

But were they fine? The three of them were in a truck with two strange men. "Where are you taking us?"

"Our mom's house; I just let her know to expect us. I have a one-room place over a garage, and Greg and his family are in a cramped mobile home. Too small for guests. Our parents have spare bedrooms."

"Isn't there a hotel nearby?" Janice didn't fancy staying with strangers. She didn't know these people and the sooner she got herself and her boys on their own the better she'd feel.

"The nearest is about an hour's drive from here. Have you looked at it out there?" Stan gestured toward the windshield.

No, she hadn't. Not much about the environment penetrated Janice's mind on their short walk from her car to this truck, and once inside, she focussed on her thawing limbs. Now, she looked through the side windows, seeing little but swirling snow. "Are we gonna be okay?"

"I've driven these roads all my life," said Greg. "And there won't be much traffic out tonight. You're lucky we came by. What were you doing out there, anyway?"

"Trying to get to Minnesota, I said, but my car broke down."

"Didn't you check the weather before heading out?"

The weather? No one checked the weather in San Diego. The weather, well, it just was. Maybe a ten-degree temperature fluctuation throughout the year, maybe three or four days of rain in the winter.

Greg spoke slowly, as if she was simple. "Minnesota weather can change quickly, and you need to check before you head out, or you could be caught in a blizzard like this one." He warmed to his topic. "And you need to be dressed properly, just in case." He nodded at the boys. "Where are the kids' snowsuits?"

"Snowsuits?" Janice couldn't seem to get all her brain cells working together.

"Yeah. You know, the clothes kids wear so they don't freeze to death out here."

"Easy, Greg," his brother warned.

"I've got kids, too. This is not how you look after them." He glanced over his shoulder at Janice. "Do you have any idea how dangerous what you did was?"

At her blank look he made a disgusted noise. "Rule number one. Check the weather to see if you should even be out on the highway. Rule number two. Have extra provisions with you - food, clothes, blankets, boots. Rule number three. Never fall asleep out in the cold. People who do, just keep on sleeping and never wake up. Do you get what I mean?"

Stan took pity on her and explained. "People freeze to death out here. If you fall asleep, the cold just seeps in, overtaking your body while you sleep, and that's it." He shook his head. She had a lot to learn if she planned to survive in Minnesota. Unless she stuck to the big cities. Maybe that was it. "Are you headed for Minneapolis?

"No. A little place called Embarrass."

"Yeah, I know it. Never been there, but it has a reputation for being the coldest place in the country." Boy, was she in for a rude awakening.

Snow muffled the sounds, cocooning them inside the warm truck cab. Nothing was visible through the side windows, other than a curtain of shifting whiteness. A faint snore came from Matt, but otherwise there was silence in the truck, other than the slap, slap of the wiper blades trying to keep the windshield clear enough for them to keep going.

Despite her best efforts to remain alert, Janice nodded off, her head resting against that of her oldest son's.

"Lady." A hand shook her shoulder. "Wake up. We're here."

Blinking, Janice looked around, her mind groggy. Cold air washed over her. To her right, Matt's car seat was empty, no sign of the child. Then, motion on her left as a man unbuckled the sleeping Alex from his seat and carried him off.

Wait! Where were these guys going with her children? That got the cobwebs from her brain and Janice scrambled across the back bench seat of the truck, frantic to find her boys.

Ahead of her stood a century-old farmhouse, complete with wrap-around porch and the requisite rockers and hanging porch swing, all snow-covered now. Lights blazed from every window and the front door stood open, despite the cold.

"Come, come along child," a man called from the door. "Hurry up and get in here. No point in trying to heat up the great outdoors. Tried that, and it never worked, not once." Seeing her struggle, he turned, slipping his feet into knee-high boots. Then, he was beside Janice, taking her arm, holding her up and spurring her on as she trudged through the deep snow. "I'll get this walk shovelled first thing tomorrow. This snow snuck up on us too fast to keep it cleared tonight."

A woman with curling grey hair waited, mostly hidden by the door. As soon as Janice and the man cleared the doorframe, she slammed the door shut behind them. "Phew.

Quite the storm, isn't it?" She didn't wait for an answer. "Come this way, dearie. I've got some hot chocolate ready for you. Can't abide coffee this time of night; I'd never get to sleep. Thought chocolate might appeal to the little ones, too, in case they woke up."

"Where are my boys?" Janice's voice got louder with each word.

"Ah, just like a momma. Come. I'll show you. We put them in the room with twin beds, thought they'd like to be near each other in case one of them woke up." She led Janice past the staircase to a small room that held two single beds and an old, painted dresser. Under crocheted quilts, Alex and Matt slumbered on. "They didn't even stir when my boys put them to bed. Kids sleep like the dead, don't they?"

Beside each bed were tiny pairs of shoes. Each boy's jacket was draped over a bed post.

The woman continued. "We didn't bother undressing them, didn't want to risk waking them up. But if you'd prefer, I'm sure we have some pajamas around here that would fit them."

"No, that's fine, thanks." Knowing that her sons were taken care of, Janice could look around, take stock of her surroundings.

The woman led her back to the kitchen. Seating at a long, wooden trestle table were the two men from the truck. Stan and Craig, or Greg, or something. With them was the other man, an older version of the brothers.

"Sit, sit." The woman waved her toward one of the mismatched ladder-back chairs. "I'll bring your chocolate in a jiffy."

Stan did the honors once again. "This is our dad, Jim,

and our mom, Phoebe." He waited. "Not sure I caught your name."

"Oh." Her brain started clicking into gear. "Janice. And my sons are Alex and Matt."

A large mug of hot chocolate appeared before her. Jim passed over a plastic bag of miniature marshmallows. "Can't have hot chocolate around here without these," he informed her.

Phoebe took a seat beside her with her own steaming mug, giving each of them a spoon. She used hers to swirl melting marshmallows around the mug. "Where are you headed?"

"Embarrass, Minnesota. Have you heard of it?"

"Heard of it? It's infamous as being the coldest spot in the continental US," said Jim. "Something about the lay of the land. The river between two mountain ranges, attracts, and traps the cold, making it sink into the valley. Sinks into your bones, too. You'll need some decent clothing to survive there." Seeing her expression, he added, "But I've heard it's pretty there in summer."

"Jim, you know as well as I do that any place is what you make of it. I'm sure this young woman here will make it the best it can be." Phoebe turned to Janice. "What takes you to Embarrass?"

"Mom, sheesh," said Stan. "Nosey much?"

"Shush, Stan. I'm just interested. Concerned." She turned to Janice, waiting.

"My boyfriend's there, waiting for us. He inherited his grandmother's house, and found a good job, so he sent for us."

"What are your plans now?"

Good question. Janice dunked a few of the marshmallows into the chocolate with her spoon. "I thought I'd drive there. It can't be much farther, is it?"

"Maybe five, five-and-a-half hours, I'd say," said Jim. "But from what the boys said, I doubt you'll be driving that car anywhere."

"Is it dead?" Please, please, say no. It's got to be okay. "It can be fixed, right?"

Greg and Stan did that sibling looking at each other thing again. "If the engine's seized, then it's dead. Putting a new engine in it might cost more than the vehicle's worth."

"It can't be seized." Whatever that meant.

"If it ran out of oil, that's bad news. Was it using oil?"

"Do you mean did I have to add oil? Yeah, I did. I tried to every time I got gas."

"Maybe there's something else going on," Jim's attempt at reassurance. "Let's not jump to conclusions until the boys tow it here in the morning."

"Tow it?" Geez, she felt like an idiot. She'd hoped that they would be able to start the thing for her, then she'd get on her way.

"We'll go get it first thing in the morning, as long as it stops snowing. Too dangerous to tow something in a snowstorm."

Phoebe patted her hand. "Let's not borrow trouble. The men will check it out in the morning, but for now, let's get some sleep. I've made up the room next to your sons for you. Or, if you'd prefer, we can move both kids into one bed together and you can have the other twin if you feel better being in the same room with them."

Janice opted for a bedroom to herself. Kids were great, especially in small doses. She needed some time to think, some time away from her sons.

Chapter Ten

Janice woke to the wafting aroma of bacon, and the excited voice of Alex, mixed with sounds from Matt. Great. The kids were up already. She pulled the pillow over her head. Just a few more minutes, please.

Thumping feet and male voices brought her to alertness sometime later. Phoebe's laughter, Alex's high-pitched voice asking his incessant questions. Janice listened. No one seemed impatient with her boys. Maybe she could sneak in just another minute or two. Goodness knows she deserved it.

Her next awareness was a knock on her door, then the squeak of the hinges as her door opened. Clutching the covers to her neck, she opened her eyes.

"No worries, it's just me," Phoebe said. "I brought you breakfast. Thought you might enjoy eating it in peace."

Janice lifted grateful eyes.

"I remember what it's like to have little ones. Always there, always needed something. And you've just been trapped together in a little car for days. You needed your sleep and a little break."

She understood. This woman got it. Janice scooted up on the bed, propping the pillows behind her back.

Phoebe set a tray across Janice's lap. A warm plate held four perfectly cooked slices of bacon, two eggs over easy, hash browns, and two pieces of buttered, wheat toast. A carafe of coffee perched on one side, with a wide mug, a small pitcher of cream and a jar of honey. Hmm. No label. Homemade?

Phoebe plunked herself near the foot of the bed and squeezed Janice's foot. "You go ahead and dig in while it's still warm." She misunderstood Janice's hesitation. "Don't worry about your boys. They've eaten. I bathed them and found fresh clothes. Greg and Stan are bundling them into snowsuits right now and will take them out to play in the snow. From the way Alex is talking, looks like your kids have never seen snow before."

Janice shook her head. "No, they haven't and neither have I."

"Believe me, you'll get over the novelty fast. The kids not so much."

Never one whose brain kicked into gear quickly when she woke up, Janice was still processing several sentences back. "Snowsuits?"

"Yep. Jim complains that I never throw anything out. He may be right about that, but I can't tell you how many times my packrat proclivities have come in handy. I have snowsuits in many sizes from when our boys were young. Greg's kids are too small to fit them yet, so your little men are welcome to them." She paused. "I take it you don't have any in your car?"

"No. I guess I hadn't thought that far ahead. It was warm when we left San Diego, in the low 70s."

"Well, it's 60 degrees colder than that here today."

What had she brought them into? Luke never mentioned cold like this when he told her about his grandmother's place. Just that it was free. A whole house to themselves. That was in August, though. Janice dipped a piece of bread into the runny yolk of an egg. "Oh, this is so good!" She looked at the bread, never tasting anything quite like it before.

Phoebe beamed. "I'm so pleased you like it. We take things for granted around here, my boys growing up with homemade bread. I use wheat we grow ourselves and grind it into flour right before I made up a batch of dough. That way it rises best. I think you can taste the freshness, the goodness, but then I might be biased."

Janice just shook her head, her mouth too full to reply. No, Phoebe wasn't wrong, not at all.

"You just tuck in there and I'll talk while you eat." She settled herself better on the bed. "Got some bad news for you. The men got the chores out of the way before daylight so they could go get your car. They towed it into the shop to work on it." She pulled one leg up underneath her. "Like they suspected, your engine is seized. It's shot. You're not going anywhere in it."

"Can it be fixed?"

"Maybe, but they say you're looking at big bucks. The boys called around. If the engine can be rebuilt, it will cost you thousands of dollars, but that's a big if. Maybe double that amount to replace it. Unless that car has huge sentimental meaning to you, it's likely not worth repairing."

Grasping the thick mug of coffee in both hands, Janice

bent her head and sipped, hoping to hide the tears that sprang to her eyes. Now what? She didn't have enough money to buy another car. The caffeine helped get her brain in gear. "Is there a bus we can take from here to Embarrass?"

Phoebe weighed her words carefully. "There is a bus in Fargo that goes to Minnesota, but only to the major cities. You could take the bus from there to Minneapolis, but you'd be almost as far away from Embarrass as you are now."

"A plane, then. Surely there's a flight we can take."

"Same thing, my dear. A flight could take you to a major city, but not anywhere near where you want to go." She let her words sink it. "What about your boyfriend? Could you ask him to come and get you? He'd make it here in five or six hours."

Her options raced through Janice's mind. If it was just her then yeah, she'd ask Luke to come get her. But he didn't know about the boys. Did she want their first meeting to take place here, in front of these people? "No, he's working."

"Surely his boss would understand. This is an emergency."

Making something up quickly, Janice said, "His truck is a two-seater. It wouldn't hold all of us."

Phoebe waited.

"I know what. There must be a car rental place in Fargo, right?"

"Yes, I imagine there is, although I've never used one. But a rental would have to be returned." She stood. "I'll be back in a minute, just go ask the boys about rentals. I'm sure they'd know."

Janice dug into the best breakfast she'd had in years.

What was it with these eggs? Eggs were eggs, right, but these tasted different, better. The yolks a vivid orange, the whites larger than usual. Perfect with this yummy bread.

Phoebe returned holding a mug of her own. "The boys already phoned around, and there are no rentals to be had. Jim says that if you want to stick around for a few days, he'll go with you to the dealerships and see if there's a decent second-hand car you could pick up for under $5000."

"$5000! I don't have that kind of money!"

"Well, you need something reliable to take off in the winter on your own with two little boys, even if it is less than a day's drive away. You can't fool around in this weather. I don't mean to frighten you, but people can die in this cold."

"Phoebe!" A male voice called from the hallway.

"Excuse me. I'll be right back."

Having wiped up every trace of egg with the delicious bread, Janice was pouring herself another cup of coffee from the carafe when Phoebe returned.

"The men have a plan." She held up her hands. "Now don't let them pressure you one way or another. The choices are entirely yours, of course. If you want to shop around for another car, you're welcome to stay here while you do so. Jim and the boys are loading cattle today, then taking them to market, but tomorrow my Jim says he can go with you to look at cars." She drank some of her coffee. "Here's another option. We have a car. It's older and hasn't been used in a few years now, but it's sound. The boys are checking it over now. They think that if they change all the oils and fluids in it, and put on its snow tires, it'll be good enough to get you where you're going."

Janice tucked her chin and looked at the older woman through lowered brows. "You'd lend me your car? You don't even know me."

SANCTUM

"Oh, child, we're not using it right now, and you look like you need one. You can return it to us once your settled, you and that young man of yours."

Chapter Eleven

Showered, dressed, and with a full stomach, Janice prepared to greet the day. So much of her life had been arranged for her while she slept and ate. Annoying, but satisfying at the same time.

Best of all, this family took care of her children for her.

Standing at the kitchen window with Phoebe, she watched her boys outside playing in the snow. Their cheeks might be redder than she'd ever seen them, but their eyes glowed as Greg showed them how to build a snowman.

Not sure it was quite her thing, all this snow, this isolation, but it certainly worked for this family. They'd made it their oasis of peace, their sanctum. Janice would do the same for her family once she arrived at Luke's.

Phoebe interrupted her thoughts. "We have a pair of boots and a winter coat for you, as well. I checked your shoe size. Your foot's a bit smaller than mine, but with an extra pair of socks, I think my boots will work for you. The coat's nothing fancy but will keep you from freezing to death."

These had got to be the givingest people she'd ever

heard of. They were strangers, opening their home to her, looking after her kids, and giving her stuff. "I'll return the clothes to you when I bring back your car, I promise."

"Not to worry. Take your time. We're only giving you things that we're not using right now." She turned back to the scene outside the window. Matt crawled along the snow. "He's bigger than his brother, but I take it he's not the oldest. How old is he?"

Janice knew which child she meant. "Almost three."

"He's delayed, isn't he?" There was no criticism in her voice.

"They say he has Sotos Syndrome. That's why he's so big for his age." She accepted another cup of coffee from Phoebe. "Thanks. Yeah, he's delayed, not meeting developmental milestones on time, according to the nurse practitioner. But he'll catch up. Kids advance at their own pace, you know."

"Oh, yes, I'm aware of that. I'm a retired special ed teacher, so I've worked with all kinds of learners." She turned to face Janice. "You know that the term 'delay' has a different meaning in psychology. If you are delayed for an appointment, that means you'll be there as you were supposed to be, but just a little late.

"When we're talking developmental delays, the meaning is slightly different. Yes, your Matt will meet the developmental milestones at his own pace, but in the meantime, his age peers will continue to move on. The pace of their learning will proceed faster than that of a child with a developmental delay, so the concept of 'catching up' doesn't really happen."

Janice pondered that. No one had explained it in that way before. She shook her head. No, that was not the way it would be for Matt. "He'll be fine by the time he reaches school age."

Phoebe wisely changed the subject. "What do you want to do now? You're welcome to stay here for a few days if you want to rest up. But if you're anxious to be on your way, we can have an early lunch, then you can leave. My boys will have tired your boys out by then, so if they eat, then they'll hopefully nap most of the afternoon, leaving you to drive in peace. You'd be at your destination by early evening."

Lunch was pulled pork sandwiches on homemade buns, with baked beans that simmered on the stove for hours. Then dessert. Alex and Matt were fascinated by the process of making ice cream, participating by adding the salt to the ice cream maker. It truly was the best dessert ever.

Jim explained that the cream came from the cows they'd milked that morning, and the pork was from a hog they'd butchered last month. The dried beans were some that Phoebe had grown in the garden last summer, and she'd soaked them overnight.

Wow. Never had Janice looked at food this way before. Food was something you picked up at the supermarket, grocery shopping just one more thing on the endless list of chores. But food came from somewhere. There were people who actually produced the stuff that ended up on the store shelves. If she and Luke had a bit of land, could they grow their own food? Thinking of the price of meat in the store, and all the other things that inflated her grocery bill, raising their own stuff could save a lot of money. People had been doing it for hundreds of years - thousands. How difficult could it be?

Jim insisted that Janice use their phone to call Luke to let him know she was getting on the road now, and the approximate time she'd arrive in Embarrass. "You can't take chances in winter. Someone needs to know where you'll be so they can come looking if you don't make it." He gave her shoulder a squeeze. "And no more sleeping in cars overnight. I'd hate for you to wake up dead."

At her expression, Jim, explained, "It's a joke. Just an expression, but you need to respect this cold. It can be a killer." He also insisted that she phone him and Phoebe to let them know she'd arrived safely at Luke's.

With their numbers written inside the cover of her travel guidebook, Janice started the borrowed car.

"Hold on," Jim said. "Looks like Phoebe's sending Stan out with something."

Stan opened the passenger seat door, putting a cooler on the floor. "Mom made you some snacks and sandwiches for supper. There are drinks in there as well." He shut the door, gave a rap on the roof of the car, and waved them off.

Chapter Twelve

A gauge on the dashboard showed the outside air temperature. Over the last hours, the number has remained in the -20s, now edging closer to -30. Thankful for the borrowed boots, they were fine inside the car. The boys slumbered peacefully, and unaided by anything other than the abundance of fresh air and good food they'd experienced.

The road sign said Virginia, Minnesota was just up ahead. Could she make it without stopping there for gas? Jim's warning sounded in her head. "Keep your tank full. If you run into trouble on the road, you might need to keep running the engine to stay warm." His other warning - "And, check the oil!"

Signaling, Janice took the exit, pulling into the first gas station she found. It was time for a potty break for her, anyway, having drained the thermos of coffee Phoebe sent with her.

The boys slept on. Good. She'd been afraid the cessation of motion would have them waking up, cranky and wanting to stretch their legs.

Gas prices were atrocious. How could it cost so much? Good thing her driving odyssey was almost over. She calculated how much she'd spend to fill up the tank. Should she? No, why should she spend her money on this? If she just waited until she got to Luke's, he'd look after such expenses from now on. She clicked off the lever and stopped filling her gas tank. Half-full was good enough. They only had another 40 minutes or so until they got there. She used her credit card to pay at the pump, then visited the restroom.

Back in the driver's seat, Janice pulled back onto the highway. Soon, soon they'd be there and start their new life together. Her sanctum. Her home.

Home. Luke. He was a good guy, and they'd had fun in San Diego. While they'd spent the night together many times, they'd not actually lived together. Janice tamped down the twinge of nervousness. It'd be fine. She was easy to get along with.

But the boys. During the long drive she'd had plenty of time to think. A part of her conscience said she should have told Luke about her sons. But when? It never seemed the right time to bring up the subject, and as time went on, well, it was awkward. Now, the time was imminent. As the car ate up the miles, she almost wished she could slow down.

This couldn't be it. Janice pulled over to read Luke's note again. She must have gotten the directions wrong. After all, there were no roads signs here to tell you the name of these snowy, dirt roads.

There was only one building on this lane, the only one

she'd seen for the last several miles. It was nothing like Phoebe's and Jim's farmhouse.

Single storey, there was no welcoming porch. Two steps led up to the door. If the siding had ever seen paint, that was a distant memory. Not even flakes remained. A small window to the right of the door had a cracked pane of glass. No shutters. No shoveled walkway, but there was evidence of a path from the side driveway to the steps. And yes, that was Luke's truck.

Yeah, maybe he had mentioned something about fixer-upper. People brought those all the time on those reality TV shows and did really well with them. It looked like fun.

But good lord. This?

Maybe there was still time to rethink this. Could she turn around and drive all the way back to San Diego? Olivia and Jerry would help. But no, she could hardly take this borrowed car all that way.

Could she return to Phoebe's and Jim's farm? They were nice people. Surely, they'd take her in for a few days while she looked for work and a place to stay.

How did she ever think this was such a good idea, driving halfway across the country for a place sight unseen? Maybe she needed to head back to the last town, Virginia, wasn't it? Have a coffee. Think about things.

Just then the front door opened. A man emerged, handling the screen door carefully as it was only attached by one of its hinges. He wore scruffy, grease-stained jeans, heavy work boots with dangling laces, and a plaid overcoat. A quilted, peaked cap was on his head, one with ear flaps hanging down and a chin strap flapping in the light breeze. Pushing the door closed, he turned to look at her.

Janice saw the man's mouth move but couldn't hear through the closed window of her car.

Now the man approached.

Could it be? No, it couldn't be. She'd never seen him wear anything more than the occasional ball cap and sweat-shirt. Was this Luke? Or maybe just some guy wondering why she was lurking outside his house.

Then he was there, pulling open her door. "Janice! I didn't recognize the car. When did you get a new one?"

Slowly she extricated herself from the vehicle. Shyness overcame her. Yes, this was the Luke she knew and loved, or at least liked quite a bit. The guy she'd driven thousands of miles to be with. The one who owned a home of his own and invited her to share it with him.

He caught her in an embrace, bruising her cold lips with a kiss. "It's been way too long since I've seen you, baby." His hug twirled her around, so she got another good look at the structure he'd emerged from.

"Is that it?" She nodded her head toward the decrepit, bare-wood building.

"Yeah, that's Granny's place, and it's all ours now." He tried to view it objectively, rather than through the lens of his six-year-old self, vacationing there with his parents all those years ago. "It needs a little work. Thought we could tackle that this summer."

Janice refrained from saying that *he'd* been here last summer. What "little work" had he done then?

Chapter Thirteen

Trying to see the place through her eyes, Luke said, "Maybe there's a bit more than a little work to do on it, but she's got good bones. A coat of paint will make a big difference. Wait until you have the yard all fixed up next year. Imagine flowers everywhere, maybe a vegetable garden. Can you imagine walking out your back door and picking strawberries? That's what it's like for some of the guys I work with. They say…"

A wail came from the back seat.

Oh, this was so not how Janice wanted to make the introductions. She needed time, time to explain to Luke, to make him see that this would all work out.

Luke bent his head to peer in the car's side window. He jerked upright. "A kid? There's a kid in the car. Where'd it come from?"

Before the words were out of his mouth, more wails were joined by words. "Mom. Mommy? Where are we? I gotta pee."

Just what she did *not* need was an accident right now.

She hurried to open the rear door and help Alex from his car seat.

"Janice," his tone cold. "Who are these kids." What he'd heard registered. "Did that one call you mom?"

Janice nodded. "Hurry. Can we get him to a bathroom quickly?"

"No! We're not moving one inch until you tell me what this is all about."

"We'll talk later. Alex needs a bathroom and fast, or you'll be sorry."

The small boy hopped from one foot to another, clutching himself, desperation his face.

"We need to settle this first. Tell him to pee outside."

Janice and Alex looked at him in horror. Janice took Alex's hand and quick-stepped him toward the sorry excuse for a house. How hard could the bathroom be to find?

Not hard. The open door and stench emanating from it led her right there. Not wanting Alex to touch anything in the filthy room, she stood close behind him while he urinated, the scrubbed his hands with the wafer of soap resting on the edge of the sink. Looking around, the only towel she could find was on the floor beside the grimy tub. She settled for wiping Alex's hands and her own on her jeans.

Sure, she'd been in Luke's bathroom at his apartment in San Diego. Never pristine by any standards, it had never rivaled a public urinal. Taking Alex's hand, she led him back out the front door.

Beside the car, Luke paced, muttering to himself. From the back seat, Matt's wails had turned to a full-on meltdown, the sort only Matt could put on. There would be no talking with Luke until Matt turned down his volume.

Janice opened the back door, unbuckling Matt from the

restrictions he fought so hard. Taking him in her arms, she felt the dampness seep into her sweatshirt through the opened zipper of her coat. Great, just great. Now *she'd* be wet and stinky as well.

Meanwhile, Alex spied the man. In his recent experience, new men meant new playmates and a newly developed skill. "Wanna make a snowman with me?"

Luke's raised brows and two backwards steps were a clear answer, even to Alex. He shrugged and bent down to the snow by himself.

Good idea thought Janice. She did up Matt's jacket, replaced the boots that had been flung off, then set him on the ground beside his older brother. They could play there while she explained things to Luke.

He waited with arms crossed, the nastiest scowl she'd ever seen on his face. "Care to explain?"

"They're my sons."

"I gathered that when the kid said 'mom'". He leaned forward, getting in her face. "Why did I never hear about them before?" He gestured toward the boys near their feet. "Slipped your mind? Forgot about them?"

"At first, I just had fun with you, liked you, and wanted to keep seeing you. Then, the timing just never seemed right, then it got harder to bring them up. I mean, how would I do that?"

"Ah, by just showing up with them. You think *that* was a better way? Don't you think it might have made a difference if I'd known you brought *kids* along with you? This changes everything." He scrubbed his face with his gloves and turned his back.

Janice laid a hand on his arm. "Luke, please. It doesn't have to change things. We're still together, that's the important thing. We're a family of four instead of two, that's all. They're good boys, easy to be around, I promise."

Matt toppled over, face first into the snow. It took several seconds for the coldness of the crusted ice pellets to penetrate his awareness. Then he let the world know of his displeasure. His shrieks drowned out Janice's last words. Bracing his body on his arms, Matt raised his face to the skies and let loose with all the angst stored up from days of being cooped up. Rivulets of tears swam down his cheeks. Copious tubes of snot ran from his nose, over his lips and down his chin, smearing on the blue of his snowsuit.

Luke averted his gaze in disgust.

Reaching down, Janice hoisted the distraught child onto her hip, some of Matt's body fluids clinging to her hair and the front of her shirt. "I've got to get the kids inside."

Luke almost gagged. He'd hugged Janice when she first stepped out of the car. Had she had grunge like that on her then? What had he touched? Gross! Then Janice's words registered. Inside? *His* house? She wanted to take these snot-nosed kids into *his* house? "Wait. We need to talk about this." No way was this happening.

Ignoring him, Janice strode to the steps, shifting the kid in the slippery snowsuit to keep him from sliding down. "Alex, come on. Time to go in."

"Noooo!" This from the other kid. "No! I'm playing. Snow."

Glancing in all directions, there didn't look to be much traffic, or any at all. Where were all the people? They'd seen no one since she got here, maybe since she turned off the highway. Alex should be okay out here by himself. It might be better to talk to Luke, get him to see reason with only one boy underfoot. One less kid would make it easier.

Chapter Fourteen

Once Matt quieted down, some of the tension eased. Putting Matt in another room helped. The child now sat at the rickety kitchen table, chowing down on one of the calzones Phoebe had sent in the cooler. Hopefully he'd be content there for a while. Food always helped with Matt.

Seeing food magically appear worked a spell on Luke. It wasn't that hard to get him to listen, with the promise of more food on the horizon. Not committing himself fully, Luke agreed that they could stay the night, maybe a few nights, while they made plans.

Janice had her plan in place. She and the boys were staying right here. Enough traveling; time to set down roots. She was tired of the diner, tired of working for a living. It was time she was taken care of. Crummy as it was, she could make this place a home for her and Luke. For the four of them.

"What are you making us for supper?" Only Luke's head and shoulders were in the kitchen. No point in getting too close to the kid perched on a tattered chair, dropping food bits all over the table.

"Depends. What have you got?" She pulled open the door to the refrigerator. Little, precious little. Beer. Ketchup. Mustard, Lidless take-out containers with remnants of what looked like Chinese food. Two slices of pizza, dried and curling on the edges, one stuck to the shelf by dried on tomato sauce. A tub of margarine. A block of cheddar with what looked like teeth marks along one edge. She opened the vegetable keeper drawer. Fuzzy stuff, stinky stuff, but nothing recognizable.

Maybe the cupboards held usable ingredients. Opening and shutting doors quickly yielded little. What a slob this guy was. He needed a full-time housekeeper. Oh, right. That's what she was. Well, there were worse things than being a homemaker and she could damn well do a better job than this. "There's nothing here to make a meal with. We need to go grocery shopping."

"We?"

"Or I can, then." A glance out the window showed Alex happy in his solitary building project in the snow. Now that Matt's initial hunger was appeased, he turned to play mode, breaking his calzone into tiny pieces spread across the table, then carefully licking up each fragment with his tongue. That would keep him occupied for some time yet, as long as no one interrupted him. Janice shoved her arms in her coat, pulling out the car keys. "Where's the nearest store?"

"In town, farther down the road. About ten miles."

"Okay. I won't be long." She was almost to the door when Luke halted her.

"Wait. What about this kid?" He pointed to Matt.

"He's fine. He'll amuse himself."

"You're not leaving *me* alone with him."

"He's fine, I said. Look, I can be there are back in half an hour and get supper started right away. If I take the boys with me, it makes everything go so much slower, and we likely won't eat for a few hours."

That gave Luke pause. He hadn't had more than a few bites of cheese and a can of beer all day. But still, she could not leave him with these brats. "I'll go with you."

Janice wrinkled her brow. Was this guy clueless? "We can't leave the kids here alone."

"You just said he's fine." His voice got louder. "Is he fine or not? What are you trying to pull?"

"What I'm *trying* to do is get stuff so that I can make us a decent meal. You have nothing in here to cook with."

Luke huffed into his bedroom, slamming the door shut. He wasn't coming out until he smelled cooked food.

Some alone time was nice, especially after the tension of Luke and the boys. Would it always be like that? Or would being with Luke mean shared parenting? Wouldn't that be great?

The highways Janice had driven on had been cleared of snow, even though the white stuff banked the ditches. This little country road was plowed all right, but not down to the ground. Janice drove on snow. Were cars supposed to do that? Maybe that's why Stan and Greg put snow tires on this car.

The grocery store wasn't in the town of Embarrass, but a different town, Babbitt. Certainly not a supermarket, but an okay selection of meat, dairy, and canned goods. A bit on the pricey side, though.

In a hurry to leave the house, Janice forgot to ask Luke for grocery money. Oh well, she could afford to pay for it now. Soon Luke would be supporting them, and she could save her money. A girl needed a stash just in case.

In the short time she was in the store, two different clerks asked her if she needed help, one asked twice. Never had that kind of service before.

And they watched her. Did they think she was going to steal something?

With her shopping cart filled with enough food to hold them for two days, Janice set her purchases on the conveyor. Now the questions started. Oh, the women were polite and hid their prying behind wide smiles, but they were nosey. What business was it of theirs who she was, where she was from, or where she was staying? This was almost as bad as being back home in Rosarito.

Except, they offered to carry her groceries to her car for her. Who does that?

Back on the road, Janice puzzled over the people in Minnesota. Weird. Maybe she'd get used to them. In the meantime, it took concentration to drive on these snow-covered roads.

She couldn't get lost. Just turn around and drive the way she'd come. But the trick was recognizing Luke's little house; it resembled several others along this road. No, wait. There was Luke's truck up ahead.

Picking up speed to make it through the drift lining the entrance to the driveway, Janice pulled in behind Luke's truck. Zipping up her coat, she braced herself for the wind that blew snow all over. Gathering the three plastic bags of food, she locked the car, pocketed the keys and trudged through the drifts toward the steps.

She stopped. What was that? Something red and grey laying across the top step, right in front of the door. She approached cautiously, until she got a clear view.

Dropping her bags, Janice ran to the still form. Alex. No movement. Still as death.

Kneeling beside him, Janice gently shook her child. Slowly Alex's eyelids fluttered. Finally, he focused, looking up at his mom with a smile. "Hungry, mom. Tired." He twisted to the side, pointing into the yard as a misshapen, two-foot pile of snow. "See my snowman?"

"Alex. Why didn't you go in the house?"

"Couldn't open the door."

"Didn't you knock."

He nodded. "And kicked, but you didn't come."

Damn that Luke. Had he left? Left Matt all alone in there? No, his truck was still here, and Luke had never been much into walking. Who would walk in weather like this?

"Come on. I bought groceries and will make us some supper." She turned the knob, but the door didn't budge. Locked? No. It took a heave with her shoulder to shove it open. Pushing Alex ahead of her, she retrieved her shopping bags and followed him inside the house.

Chapter Fifteen

No sign of Luke. Opening the bedroom door, Janice saw him. Arms and legs outstretched, he sprawled across the bed. Empty beer cans littered the bedside table, some upright, some on their sides, stuck to dried puddles of dregs.

Wrinkling her nose, Janice withdrew, shutting the bedroom door behind her. If Luke could fall sleep despite the stench in that room, he shouldn't object to any odors Matt created. Yeah, this would work out.

Soon the aroma of caramelizing onions mixed with a hint of garlic replaced smells of lousy housekeeping and poor personal hygiene. This would be the best meal Luke had eaten since he left San Diego. Janice only had a few cooking tricks up her sleeve, but chili was one of them.

But it took time, and the kids were getting restless. Again. Remembering that angel, Phoebe, Janice donned her boots and ran to the car for one of the bags that woman had placed in the car. Coloring books and crayons. Puzzles, building blocks. That woman thought of everything. For now, the coloring books and crayons kept the boys busy.

Matt's fisted grip moved the crayons in erratic motions, but Janice doubted Luke would even notice the new marks now decorating his stained table.

Groans and creaking bedsprings. Ah, Luke was waking up, likely aided by the wafting aroma of simmering chili.

He made his way to the kitchen, ignoring the boys and put his arms around Janice. His hands inched up her chest.

She slapped them away, giving Luke a dirty look. "The boys are here."

"So?" He glanced at the table where two little heads bowed over their artwork. "They don't care."

"*I* do." She'd need to set sound ground rules and make it clear that she was boss inside this house. Things would happen when and where she decided.

Luke retreated. He could wait. "When do we eat?"

"About ten minutes. Would you toss the salad?"

"What? Me? I don't know anything about that." He backed out of the room. "Call me when its ready." He plunked himself into a sagging chair in the living room, adding, "Smells good."

Doesn't know how to toss a salad? Or won't do it. Another thing we'll need to work on, thought Janice. She opened the packet of Caesar dressing and mixed it into the bowl of lettuce. Good thing she'd bought a ready-made salad, unsure if Luke even had a salad bowl. This plastic one could be washed and reused.

She opened the oven door to check on the thick slabs of toasting bread, slathered with garlic butter and grated cheese. Almost done.

"Boys, put your books away and go wash your hands."

"Where?" Alex asked.

Good question. Turning the oven's broiler off, she picked up Matt, carrying him into the bathroom. She grimaced. What a disgusting room. Their hands might get dirtier washing in here. She sighed and stuck the child's hands under the flowing water anyway, and scrubbed them with the grimy, cracked bar of soap. She couldn't bring herself to use any of the towels littering the floor, so used Matt's shirt tail to dry the child's hands.

Behind her, Alex watched, then stretched on tiptoes to wash his own hands. Shaking them off, water flew everywhere, but what did it matter? No one would even notice Alex's contribution to the mess in this bathroom.

"Go tell Luke it's supper time," she told Alex.

"Who?"

"The man in the living room."

Alex planted himself squaring in front of Luke, obstructing the television.

"Hey, move, kid."

"Mister, Mom says it's supper time."

"Why didn't you say so?"

Puzzled, "I did."

The food was excellent, thought Luke. Best things he'd eaten in months. Should he tell Janice? Wouldn't want it to go to her head or anything. Maybe with this kind of cooking, she could stay, even if it meant having the brats underfoot. She could keep them away from him, couldn't she?

Slowly, something else penetrated his senses - an odor unrelated to the meal he was stuffing into his mouth. Had someone farted? Luke glanced at Janice, but she wielded her fork, unaware. Luke frowned and looked at the boys. Could bodies that small be responsible for a such a foul smell?

"Mom, he's done it again," Alex informed them. "He stinks."

True. Janice could ignore it no longer. Working at keeping her face's expression neutral, she hoisted Matt from where he knelt on a chair.

Matt protested, not ready to leave his meal.

Unheeding her son's growing squawks, Janice carried him to the bedroom.

"Hey," called Luke. "That's my room. What are you doing?"

Just one more thing to ignore. Males of the species could be annoying. She dropped Matt onto the bed. "Stay there," she ordered Matt. "Don't move." Yeah, as if that ever worked. She retrieved the diaper bag from where she'd left it by the door.

Gross. This was an especially bad one. Matt was worse when he ate irregularly, or too much junk food. Well, it couldn't be helped if she was to get them to Minnesota. Now that they were here and had a home, she'd do better. She looked around the bedroom. A home, such as it was.

Footsteps behind her, far too heavy to belong to Alex. Besides, that kid knew to come nowhere near his brother during a diaper change. Alex's instinct for self-preservation was strong.

A sound or retching came from the doorway, then those same steps running to the bathroom. Then more retching.

Served him right. No one invited him to the diaper change party.

Where else was she supposed to change Matt, if not on the bed? The living room couch? The kitchen table?

Then it dawned on Janice. She hadn't noticed a second bedroom. Where would the boys sleep?

Chapter Sixteen

An uneasy truce took over the little household. Neither adult mentioned the presence of the boys, Luke choosing to ignore them. After all, decent meals were served to him, he no longer had to cringe when entering the pig sty his bathroom had disintegrated to, and Janice, well she had other assets, ones he'd not sampled since he left San Diego last summer. That made up for the nuisance of having rug rats around. As long as she kept them out of his way, this might work.

Except that she made him keep the TV down low in the evenings. Granted, it was pleasant that she put the kids to bed early, but even that cramped his style.

The first night, Janice made a nest for the boys using towels (he didn't tell her they were all dirty), placing them in a corner of the kitchen floor. Yeah, she was right. The alternatives were to share a bed with them. Shudder. What if that kid crapped himself again? Or the living room couch. But then Janice made a big deal about no noise from the

TV, or even talking, in case they woke the kids up. She assured him that he wouldn't like that.

He got it. He'd seen several episodes already of the kids squawking, especially the one who couldn't walk yet. What was up with that? Janice hadn't spoken to him for the rest of the day the one time he'd asked what was wrong with the kid, and she withheld her charms that night. He didn't make *that* mistake again.

Gradually, the little house took shape. The bathtub received a cursory scrub that first night so the boys could have a bath, but in the coming days, it got better. Janice complained lots about it, how it was impossible to get clean, how the stains would never come out, how they needed a replacement tub. Like *that* was going to happen. The woman had no idea how much work that would be, nor how much money it would take. Did she think he had bags of dough?

And she nagged. She wanted the bathroom towels hung up on the towel bars. *Every* time. She was some sort of fanatic about it.

She wanted him to rinse away his hairs every time he took a razor to his chin. Solved that one, though. He stopped shaving. Besides, the whiskers helped keep his face warmer in the godforsaken place.

At first when she started asking for grocery money, it felt sort of good to be the provider, to doll out the cash in bits at a time. But soon she demanded more - more than for just food. She wanted new towels. She wanted beds for her kids. Beds? Where did she think she was going to put beds? No way were they going in his living room.

In the end, she settled on small, blow-up air mattresses. In the day, they went in the back closet, the one she said was supposed to hold coats and boots. Who would do that? That meant traipsing through the entire house to get back there. Nah, it was more efficient to throw your coat over the chair by the front door and your boots beside the door that you'd be using. Right?

Janice insisted that they buy a boot mat. Then two of them, saying that one wouldn't hold four pairs of boots. Four? That was never his intention, so she'd just have to deal with it.

She wanted blankets and pillows for her kids to use on the air mattresses. That damned Janice threatened to take the quilt off *his* bed and give it to the kids if he didn't cough up the money for bedding. Yeah, she kept him warm at night, but not *that* warm.

All this demand to buy things burned through his savings quickly. Yeah, the meals were good, but did they have to cost so much? This was far more than he used to spend on food, even considering that he ate mostly take-out food. Must be the extra mouths. Not only did the snot-nosed kids take up space, but they cost money.

Money. Time to talk to Janice about the plan. She seemed to be settling into the Suzie Homemaker role, but he had other plans.

"No, you can't have more money. Where do you think money comes from?" Sheesh. Yet another demand that he spend his hard-earned cash on her and her brats. Wasn't it enough that he provided a roof over their heads? Time to get real.

"Here's the deal," he said. "My job is seasonal. It's good money in the summer, and okay money spring and fall. But there's almost no work in the winter."

"But…"

Luke didn't let her finish. "See, that's where you come in. While I'll bring in the main bucks much of the year, you'll take up the slack in the winter months. You need to get a job."

"But I thought…"

"What? What exactly did you think? That you could sit on your butt around here and that I'd do all the work? That I'd take on you and these brats you thought you'd slip by me? Thought I was some chump?"

"No, that's not how it is…"

"Damned right it isn't. I provide you with a free place to live, but there are other bills, lots of them, and those two…" he gestured toward the boys, "…are a big part of the problem. They're your responsibility, yet you try to make them mine. Well, I've had enough of this. You need to get your ass into town and get yourself a job."

"If I go to work, who will look after Alex and Matt?"

"How should I know? Not my problem. Deal with it." He put on his coat and boots. "Nancy at the diner is looking for help. I already spoke to her; told her you'd be in." He straightened, staring into her eyes through lowered brows. "Don't screw this up."

Chapter Seventeen

As she viewed the last of San Diego in her rearview mirror, Janice had believed her days of working in a diner were over.

Not so much.

Nancy, owner of the Best Ever Diner in Embarrass hired her on the spot. After trying a revolving door of high school kids and senior citizens who could only work certain hours, Nancy wanted a waitress who could work full shifts. That Janice had experience was a bonus.

No reference checking. No paperwork. Nancy assured her this was the best way for Janice to keep all of her minimum wage salary, with none of those pesky government deductions. "Trust me. You'll have more money in your pocket this way."

More money would be good, and it's not like Janice would be contributing to a 401K anyway.

There was one niggly little problem, though. "Is there a daycare in this town?"

"There are a few women who look after kids in their homes, but not a daycare center."

"Any idea how much they charge?"

"Not sure. The last I heard, it was around $2 an hour."

"Per kid?"

Nancy shrugged. Not her problem.

If it was per kid, then Janice would be in the hole. Her $3.50 an hour wage would be eaten up even if she just paid someone to look after Matt.

No, if he wanted to see any of her money, then Luke would have to look after the boys while she worked. It's not like he was doing anything else, anyway. How hard could it be?

Quite hard, apparently.

Janice's first day of work began at 7 a.m. the next morning. Getting ready as quietly as she could, Janice slipped out of the house while Luke and both boys slept. Luke she could have handled, but life would have been complicated if Matt or Alex woke, needing her attention.

She forgot about warming the car up. What a weird concept. Here, you couldn't just jump in the car and go. When Phoebe and Jim loaned her their car, they'd given her a lesson in waiting until the car's temperature gauge needle moved to the right, off the C mark.

Shivering, she sat in the car waiting. How long before the stupid thing decided to move? She'd freeze if she sat here much longer. Returning to the house to wait was not an option. What if one of the boys woke up? That would totally mess up her plans.

She put the car in gear and steered down the narrow, white road, praying she stayed on the track to town.

Thank God she had this car. Yeah, it was a loaner, and the deal was that she'd return it as soon as she got to Luke's.

But how was she supposed to do that? Luke's truck was a two-seater, so couldn't hold all of them. And how would she get to work? Luke's truck was an ancient stick shift. Who knew how to drive something like that? Besides, even if she could figure out how to shift gears, Luke wouldn't let her touch his truck, said he needed his wheels in case he wanted to go somewhere.

Maybe after she'd worked enough, saved up some money, she could buy a car of her own, then she could return Jim and Phoebe's car to them.

Waitressing was the same old, same old. Stuff was stored in different places, but the routine was the same.

Same smells, too. The aroma of slightly burnt coffee scorched into the bottom of the carafe. The scent of several days old grease hanging in the air, mixed with that of freshly buttered toast.

The difference was that here everyone knew one another. None of the anonymity of the city, everyone wanted to know who she was, where she was from and her connection to this town. After the dozenth time, Janice recited her story by rote. She got it. It was a small town, not unlike Rosarito where she grew up, with nosy people who couldn't mind their own business.

Alex put his eye to the crack in the bedroom door. "Mommy, Matt's hungry."

No response.

Turning the knob, he stuck his head in. A hairy foot stuck out of the covers. There was one lump on that side the bed, but no mom.

Braving this grumpy man's wrath, he approached. The man was still, other than his lips moving in and out as he snored.

"Mister, hey mister." Alex shook the guy's shoulder. "Where's Mommy?"

The guy grunted and rolled over.

From the kitchen came those noises, the ones Matt started with when he was working up to a meltdown.

Alex tried again, this time using his fist on the guy's arm.

"Leave me alone, kid. Go away." The snoring started again with a snort.

"I need my mom. Matt's hungry. And he needs a new diaper."

"GO AWAY! Your mother's at work. Now get out of here."

Luke rolled over in bed. Hard to get any sleep with those bratty kids rummaging around. No consideration. He'd have to talk to Janice about teaching those kids some manners. And rules. They needed rules around here.

Sure, it was one thing if the boys wanted to get themselves some cereal from the cupboard, but did they have to drag the chair across the floor to do it?

A pillow over his head helped drown out the ruckus in the kitchen, and soon enough his snores covered up everything else.

———————

Work. Alex knew about that. When Mommy'd go to work, he and Matt stayed with Olivia and Jerry. Unless they were in bed, then Mom said to stay there until she came home.

But she hadn't said anything about work, or what to do when they woke up. Was this man supposed to look after them? He wasn't a very nice man, not like Jerry, who played with them, and gave them hugs.

Matt scooted on his bum to get to his big brother.

Mom hated it when Matt did that, especially first thing in the morning. She said it mushed everything around in his diaper, making him harder to clean.

Just in case the man was lying, Alex checked the bathroom. No Mom. Her boots weren't by the door, either.

His stomach rumbled. They hadn't lived here very long, but he knew where Mom kept the cereal. Using both hands, he pulled a chair across the floor so he could climb onto the counter to reach the upper cupboards. It was a big step from the chair to the countertop, but by lying on his stomach, he was able to swing his legs up, then stand on the counter.

He found what he needed in the second cupboard. It was hard balancing up so high, standing near the edge to open the doors. Then he had to reach inside to grab the boxes.

Oops. The corn flakes box toppled to the corner of the counter, bounced, then hit the floor, spilling its contents. That was okay. Matt waited there and stopped his noises as he scooped up handfuls of the dry cereal, munching away.

Good thing he was fine with it dry because Alex tried to pull open the fridge door but wasn't strong enough. He joined Matt on the floor and ate breakfast.

Although used to the smell, Alex could not stand it any longer. The grumpy man was awake now and watching TV. Alex waited until the guy had a coffee cup in his hand.

Mom told them never to bother her before she had her coffee.

"Mister, Matt stinks."

"You've got that right. What does your mother feed the kid?"

"He needs his diaper changed."

Luke took his gaze from the television and looked Alex up and down. "So, change it then. Why are you telling me?"

"I've never changed a diaper before."

"You think *I* have?"

Alex wrinkled his brow. "But grownups do it."

"Don't look at me. Not my problem." The odor of a dirty diaper wafted Luke's way as Matt bum-scooted closer. "You change it. He's your brother."

As Alex turned away, Luke added, "And keep that stink away from me."

Chapter Eighteen

Her feet. Janice forgot what it was like to be on her feet all day. Before leaving San Diego, she tossed her waitressing shoes, vowing never to need such things again. Mistake.

At least the heater in this borrowed car worked; maybe not at first, but by the time she reached Luke's house, it was a decent temperature in her little bubble. Parking, she regarded the house. Not her image of a charming farmhouse, but Luke said they could make something of it come summer. Maybe.

With the dying sunlight glinting off the snow, it was sort of pretty here, in a weird way. She'd lost all her romantic notions of snow.

You're stalling, she told herself. True, so true. Who knew what confronted her once she entered that little house? Exhausted from her first shift at work, she had a feeling her day was not over yet.

Her attempt at a cheery face fell away instantly. Luke's bare feet dangled over the side of the armchair. The television announcer roared with glee over some hockey goal.

Dirty dishes littered the floor and the top of the TV. Thank goodness the bedroom door was closed.

From the front door Janice could see into the kitchen. The floor was covered in crumbs or food, with some of it stretching onto the living room carpet. There. An over-turned corn flakes box. That accounted for the crumbs.

"What did you feed the kids?" Janice asked Luke.

"Me? They're not my kids. You feed them if you want them fed. And while you're at it, teach them to clean up after themselves." He gestured toward the open kitchen doorway. "Have you seen the mess they made?"

"No. I just got home after working all day."

Either Luke missed the point of her comment or chose to ignore it.

She tried again. "I don't suppose you've made supper?"

"Me? I don't cook. You said you were good at that." His attention returned to the TV. "I could use something to eat, though." He balled up a potato chip bag. "These don't hold me that well."

Hearing her voice, Alex ran to his mom, Matt skidding along the floor behind him. Both extended their arms to be picked up. It had been a while since Alex had done that, maybe almost a year. What had the day been like to cause him to regress to a more infantile reaction? She hugged him to her side.

As Janice reached to pick up Matt, his scent filled her nostrils. Filled was the operant word. Good Lord. "Has no one changed this kid's diaper?"

Luke ignored her.

"*I* did!" This from Alex. "It was gross, really, really gross."

Janice looked more closely at Alex's shirt. Suspicious brown streaks ran down the front and arms. And yes, there were blotches on his pants as well. She averted her gaze from Matt. If Alex changed him and looked like this, what shape would the younger one be in?

More laundry. For now, a bath. A bath would keep the kids occupied while she cleaned up enough to get some food going.

Not daring to hold Matt close to the clothes she'd need for work again tomorrow, Janice instructed the boys to follow her. Her feet scrunched on the remnants of the spilled cereal all over the kitchen floor. Picking up the over-turned cereal box, she found it empty. Sigh. She'd need to buy more. What a waste. So much trampled food on the dirty floor.

She halted at the doorway to the bathroom. Dried excrement caked parts of the tub, and smeared trails over the floor. Soiled diapers lay tossed along the bathroom wall. More brown bits lined the edge of the sink and the taps.

Outside sat the still-warm car. She could get in it and just drive until she could see no one, vanish into the evening air on her own. No one bugging her, no one depending on her.

As a single mom, often Janice felt like running. Surely there had to be more to life than this drudgery? Why did everything have to be so hard? The urge to flee had never been as strong as at this moment.

A grubby hand tugged on the side of her pants. "Mom, Mom. I looked after Matt all by myself."

Yeah, she could see that. She looked into his beaming face and swallowed the words that came to her throat. Not his fault. He didn't get them into this mess. Not his fault that he had such a shitty life.

Shit, no kidding.

Okay. One thing at a time. "Stay there. Don't move."

Striding to the bedroom, she removed her pants and shirt. She could not clean that bathroom wearing her work clothes. Rummaging in her suitcase, she found the oldest clothes she owned.

Luke came in just then. "Hey, babe." He eyed her form in a bra and panties and reached for her.

Janice evaded his hands.

Her back-off look overrode any plans her unclothed state inspired in Luke's mind.

Turning her back, Janice donned her clothes and brushed past him.

Taking cleaning supplies from under the sink, Janice tackled the tub first. The porcelain lost its pristine potential decades ago. Now she aimed only to erase the brown chunks and streaks.

"Hey," came from the living room. "Be careful how much water you're using. The well only holds so much and I need a shower later."

She ignored him. Putting in the plug, she filled the tub, adding a few dabs of dish soap to create bubbles. What could it hurt? And the kids loved bubbles.

Janice tried to breather through her nose while she removed Matt's clothing. He cooperated, knowing a bath was in his near future. Alex shed his own clothes, clambering into the tub on his own.

Gathering the dirty diapers, Janice tossed them in the garbage under the kitchen sink. She'd ask Luke to take out the trash after he'd eaten. Surely, he could do that much.

Next, she planned to return to the bathroom to grab the kids' dirty clothes but could not stand how her feet crunched through the cereal on the floor. So much to do. It was hard to prioritize.

Reaching for the ancient, frayed broom and dustpan behind the door, Janice began the chore of sweeping the mess from the floor, angling the dustpan into the trash can with each load. She stopped at the edge of the carpet. That ground-in stuff was another day's job.

Now, food. How was she supposed to make a meal when the countertop was full of dirty dishes? It looked like someone had burnt a can of baked beans into a pot, scraping the useable bits onto a plate, then leaving the refuse to harden on. There were toast crumbs. An open jar of peanut butter, with the knife used to spread the stuff stuck to the counter.

She'd need to clean this mess up before she had space to cook.

Luke raised his voice to be heard over the TV. "Babe, when's dinner?"

She left California for this?

Chapter Nineteen

Unable to face coming home from work the next day to the mess created by the kids, it would be better for all of them if the boys slept much of the time. Thank goodness she'd thought to buy an extra bottle of Children's Benadryl.

As for the mess Luke would make, well, there was not much to be done about that. At least he was toilet trained, although she had to wonder about some of the spillage around the toilet bowl.

Alex, semi-proficient at dressing himself, figured out how to stuff his brother into a snowsuit and boots so they could go outside to play. It was better than staying in the house with nothing to do but get yelled at by that man.

Several times Janice got home from work to find the boys asleep, piled together on the doorstep. Once they buried a hole in the snow, a nest Alex called it, and had a nap there.

"Aren't you cold?" Janice asked.

Alex shook his head. Watching, Matt copied his brother.

From her years waitressing, Janice had learned to remove her mind from her job. Once she knew where everything was stored and how Nancy liked things run, she could operate on automatic.

Too bad, she thought. It gave her too much time to brood. Maybe if she had a job that occupied her mind, she'd be better off. One day....

Luke hinted all the time how much better off they'd be, just the two of them. It wasn't really hinting. It was more like stating. He never hid his irritation at having the kids around.

Luke felt Janice was unreasonable. She demanded too much from him. These weren't his kids; kids were never part of the equation. If he'd wanted kids, he would have had kids. It wasn't his fault if she tried pawning them off on him.

True. Jerry and Olivia had warned her. But she'd been so sure that Luke wanted her badly enough that the surprise addition of two little boys would not be a problem once the initial shock wore off. Not so much, it seemed.

Yeah, Luke still wanted her, at least in the bedroom department. That was good, except for the days when she was bone-weary from being on her feet all day. Luke said he didn't want her on her feet and laying down was just fine.

He also wanted her money. He boasted of the abundant cash he'd bring in next summer, with lots of overtime. If that was true, where was the money he'd earned last summer?

She was being too hard on him, Luke said. He had

needs. While the house came rent-free, there were still expenses and repairs she didn't understand.

What Janice did understand was parenting. Motherhood had not come easy to her, and she'd had over half a year to get her mind around the fact that Alex would be arriving. Then, two years later, came Matt, amplifying her mothering chores.

To be fair to Luke, he'd been blind-sided by this whole family thing. No time to wrap his mind around it. No time to gradually adjust to a tiny being turning into a toddler.

Luke was right, though. The boys were a lot of work. They also cramped their style, costing them in food and clothes, and preventing them from going out partying.

That weekend, Luke got a call from his boss. Saturday's storm blew down trees all over the county and their tree-removal services were needed. There would be at least two, maybe three days' work.

"But what about the boys?"

"Not my problem," Luke replied. "What? Don't you want me to earn money? I'll make double what you do in a day."

That wasn't the problem. Leaving the boys alone was. It's not that she'd never done it before, but Olivia and Jerry had been in the next apartment in case of, well, just in case. Alex knew how to go to their place and get them if needed. Besides, she only left them alone once they were asleep. During the day was different.

"Maybe I should take them to a babysitter."

"And waste all that money? You said it would cost more than you make. Doesn't that defeat the purpose of having a job?"

"You just said you'll make double what I do."

"Sure, but that's not a regular thing, not until summer anyway."

"I'm just not sure…"

"Give them some of your sleepy-time juice."

But how to give it to them? Usually, the boys were asleep when she left for work. She could hardly wake them up to dose them. Besides, waking Matt up before he was ready spelled disaster for everyone.

She put two plastic glasses of "juice" on a low shelf in the cupboard, making sure Alex knew where to find them for breakfast the next morning. Just a little bit of grape juice mixed with water and the medicine would do the trick.

Since that first disastrous day, she'd learned to set out bowls of cereal for the boys in that same accessible cupboard. The kids could not be trusted to pour milk, so they ate it dry.

Behind the cereal bowls were two sandwiches ready for their lunch. Maybe they'd get a bit dried out by then, but they were better than nothing. Both boys liked peanut butter and jelly, so it was a win-win for everyone. Maybe she wouldn't get Mother-of-the-Year award, but they were fed.

Chapter Twenty

Good thing there was a pharmacy in town. Janice made several trips there, replenishing her supply of Children's Benadryl.

One day the pharmacist stopped her. "Looks like you're buying a lot of that stuff."

"Can't be too careful," Janice said. "Got a kid with allergies."

"What's he allergic to?"

"Bee stings." That was the first thing that popped into her head.

The pharmacist glanced out the front window at the banked snow. "Haven't noticed that the bees were that active this time of year."

"No, that's just his worst allergy. He reacts to all sorts of things. Like dust. Yeah, dust. I work full-time, so it's hard to keep the house as clean as I should. He reacts, so this helps." She held up a bottle of the medicine.

"Is your child over age 2?"

"Yes. They both are."

The pharmacist raised his eyebrows. "You have *two* allergic children?"

"Yes, I mean no. I have two sons. One is sickly." At least that much was true.

"How much does he weigh?"

"About 45 pounds."

"So that means he shouldn't have more than 7.5 ml at a time, and no more than once every four to six hours."

"Oh, I only give it once in a day." She thought a moment. "Well, maybe I've done it twice, but that's it."

"That's good because there can be side effects with this medication. Serious ones like seizures, hallucinations, heart problems. But I imagine your doctor has discussed all this with you."

Janice nodded.

The pharmacist reached for another box on the shelf. "It also comes in a chewable form if that makes it easier. At his weight, he could have one tablet."

"Thanks, I'll keep that in mind." She turned to walk away. "For now, I'll stick with what's working."

That evening, after the boys were asleep on their pallets on the kitchen floor, Janice told Luke about her encounter with the pharmacist. "We'll need to go shopping somewhere else this weekend, to a bigger town to buy more. This guy sounded suspicious about why I was buying this stuff so often."

Luke sighed. "Just one more problem those kids of yours cause us." He flipped channels with the remote. "It just never stops with them, does it?"

Alone in the shower, Janice let the tears rain down her face. Resting her forearms on the wall, she let the sobs out. For so long she'd been strong. For more than four years, since she learned she was first pregnant. Alone, she'd done it all. And for what?

People said it got easier once the baby stage for over. Or when the terrible twos were gone. Or when the kids walked or talked or were potty-trained. No, it hadn't gotten easier. Different, but not easy. No, never easy.

She thought that having a partner would make it all better. But that wasn't the answer, either. She had Luke, that was a good thing. How many times had her mother drummed it into her head the importance of finding a man to look after you?

But even with Luke, life remained the same drudgery it was before. She could see her days stretching endlessly - the same treadmill, the same constant demands, the same chores, the same non-stop need for her attention. When was there "me" time?

Weariness and despair settled into her bones, filling every crevice, and fusing her sinews with cement.

The water grew cold. The ancient hot water tank didn't have much oomph left. Janice turned off the taps, grabbing a bath sheet she'd purchased last week. Her one indulgence. Why did a girl have to feel guilty buying herself a decent towel? Luke said she could have bought him one, too, if she didn't have to buy new mittens for those kids who'd lost theirs yet again.

"They really cut into our life, you know," he'd complained.

True. It was all true.

But what about from the kids' points of view? Yeah, this might be the only life they knew, but it wasn't great, by any standards. Left to their own devices all day, five or six days a week. Living in this shack. Barely any toys. A father figure who hollered at them and acted like he hated them. A mother too exhausted to meet more than their basic needs, if that.

Face it. She was not a good mother. It's not like she didn't try; she did, she really did. But it was all just so hard, hard for her and hard for her boys. Not much of a life for any of them.

Janice wiped off the vanity mirror with the edge of her towel. Were those crow's feet? Was she developing lines in her face? She hadn't even lived the first third of her life yet and already she was looking like a hag.

She stifled her sobs. No more tears. Now that the shower was off, she couldn't risk waking the boys, or letting Luke see her cry. He needed to believe she was happy to be with him. She couldn't risk him kicking her out. She no longer had friends nearby to fall back on, friends like Olivia and Jerry.

That reminded her. She felt her breasts. Olivia used to be a nurse on a women's ward. She preached non-stop about the importance of breast self-examination, having seen too many women succumb to breast cancer because they hadn't checked themselves regularly.

How long had it been since she'd done this? Ages. Maybe not since she left San Diego. Olivia would lecture her if she knew.

Carefully feeling the right breast, she worked in a quadrant pattern, the way Olivia taught her. Switching hands, she moved to the left breast. What? What was that? It felt almost the size of a marble. She could move it around, under her skin. That hadn't been there before. Standing up straighter, she felt some more. No, nothing else, just that same roundish thing, a lump that shouldn't be there.

For the next week, Janice went through the motions of existing. She got up while everyone slept, got breakfast and sandwiches ready for Luke and the boys before leaving the house. She drove to work and put in her time there. Drove home. Cleaned and cooked and fell into bed.

A lump. A lump in her breast. The same breast that felt sore from all the handling and pushing and prodding she'd done. Was it cancer? Was she pushing those cancer cells around by poking at the lump? Of course it was cancer. What else could it be?

They had no medical insurance, neither of them. They also had no spare cash to pay for a doctor's appointment, let alone the thousands and thousands of dollars it would take for the treatments to fight breast cancer.

No, they just couldn't do it.

How long did she have? Did people die quickly of breast cancer? Was she looking at months? Years?

Would she be around to see her boys grow up? Doubtful. Not from what Olivia had said, anyway. She talked about so many young women dying from this disease.

If she died, what would become of her boys? Luke wouldn't take care of them. He couldn't, or wouldn't, even when she was here to do most of the heavy lifting. Alone, he'd never do it, wouldn't even try.

She couldn't ask Olivia and Jerry to take them. They were old and retired. While they made great grandparent substitutes, they had their own grandkids. Besides, they were half a country away.

Phoebe and Jim? They were virtual strangers, despite their kindness. Besides, she'd pretty much stolen their car. They would not want to hear from her, other than to get their vehicle back.

Let the boys become wards of the state? No good things

happened to kids in foster homes, at least that's what she'd always heard. There was a reason so many movies are made about atrocities kids went through once they became part of the system.

No, the boys were her responsibility. She brought them into this world. Their fate was in her hands.

Chapter Twenty-One

A large envelope came from Olivia. The dear woman included a note saying this was all of Janice's mail she'd collected since Janice and the kids left. She wasn't sure she'd got all of it since there was a new tenant in Janice's old suite and he chucked in the trash anything that wasn't his.

Olivia gently reminded Janice that she might want to have the post office forward her mail, change her address with her creditors.

Just one more thing to get around to.

Within the envelope was her Visa statement. Never good, but at least she kept up with the minimum payments on it. She'd hoped that with Luke supporting them, she could make some headway on the principle. Fat chance now. Skimming the pages, most charges were expected, things like gas, hotels and food during their drive. But one leapt out. An outrageous amount from that lovely hotel in Vegas. Why were they charging her twice? More than twice? She'd paid the hotel bill and only stayed there one night.

This was not right. They'd made a mistake, a costly one. Although Luke hated long-distance charges on his phone bill, this call would be worth it.

Janice slowly set the phone back in its cradle. So. Those snacks in the minibar had not been complimentary. Damn! They cost more than the hotel room's charge.

Yeah, she'd had a few drinks from the minibar. Well, maybe she'd consumed all the alcohol the tiny fridge offered. But the snacks - most of those she'd fed to the boys.

They might be just kids, but they ate a lot. Feeding them cost more than it did to feed herself. She mentally calculated how much more money she'd have if she only bought groceries for herself.

Luke was right; kids burned through your cash.

Driving home from work Janice fingered her left breast, praying that the lump had disappeared, a figment of her imagination. Stuff healed, right?

But no, it was still there. Was it bigger? No, impossible. The thing couldn't grow larger in a week. How fast did tumors spread anyway?

Enough. She was tired and couldn't dwell on the impending doom of her health.

But the negative part of her brain wouldn't let up.

Maybe when facing the end of life, past stuff flooded your brain. She thought of her early years, growing up in Rosarito with her mother Elena.

"Find a man to look after you. Life is too hard for a woman alone," Elena preached.

While her mom truly believed what she said, finding that perfect man eluded Elena. Janice's father was still around. Sort of. They'd see him around town, mostly drunk and stumbling, or loud and obnoxious in the cantina.

Sometimes he recognized Juana, sometimes not. That was fine; she pretended not to recognize him, either. Who wanted a father who loved his booze more than he did his little girl?

But if nothing else, Elena persisted in her dream. She went from man to man, trying to find that perfect one to support her and her family. Some stayed only a few days; a couple remained fixtures in their little house for years. Some contributed to the household income; many lived off Elena. But in the end, they all left.

Janice would not be like that. She'd found Luke, a man who wanted her, a man who sent her money to come live with him. Sure, it was a bit disappointing once she arrived, but his job was seasonal. Once this everlasting winter ended, he'd bring home good money and living would be easy.

Taking in the white scenery around her drove home the fact that this was winter. Still early February, and in this part of the country, spring was still a few months off, let alone summer.

She felt her left breast again. Would she even be here come summer?

The sniffles started again. No. She wiped her nose on her sleeve. No way did she have time for that, time to feel sorry for herself. She had responsibilities, plans to make.

Elena might live life with her head in the clouds, always believing the right man was just around the corner. Huh. Like that would ever happen.

Janice prided herself on being a realist. Lie to others, but never to yourself.

No, she was not going to be around much longer. She needed to prepare.

Her father might have ditched his kids without a thought, but she was not like that. She had children and needed to think of their future.

Her shoulders sagged. No sense in beating herself up over what their life had become. She'd tried, tried her best. If it wasn't good enough, it wasn't good enough. Now she needed to do what was right for them.

Life in the state system would be a hell from which the boys would never escape. Without her around, Luke would never look after them.

Two small boys, not yet school-age, one with extra problems, would not survive in this world. They were her responsibility. She brought them into this world and should have a say in how they leave it.

A plan formed. A desperate one, an audacious one, but then, Janice prided herself on taking bold moves when needed.

Running through her head were the warnings from Jim and Phoebe and their sons. Warnings about how easy it was to freeze to death in these Minnesota winters, how falling asleep in the cold might be the last thing you ever did.

Was that better for the boys? Falling gently asleep and never waking up again, never suffering what fate had in store for them without a mother?

Chapter Twenty-Two

It didn't take much to convince Luke that this was the best way out of their problems. As long as he didn't get caught, Luke was fine with the plan. Finally, it would be just the two of them. His subtle and not so subtle hints over the past weeks paid off.

They didn't travel to another town to purchase more Benadryl on the weekend. They wouldn't need much more and had enough for their purposes.

Janice made a nice meal Saturday night, the boys' favorite. Hot dogs and beans. She even carved up some carrot sticks. Veggies were good for you.

Taking his cue from Janice, Luke voluntarily addressed the boys for the first time ever. "Your mom and I have a surprise for you." He infused his voice with more enthusiasm. "We're going to play in the snow."

"Yay!" Alex yelled, with Matt giving his best imitation of the cheer.

Janice carefully washed the boys faces and hands, showing all the maternal care she could muster. "And here's some of your favorite juice." She helped Matt with his cup, taking care that every drop made it down his throat. She's spooned extra sugar into the concoction to make it extra appealing. She gently shoved the little boy's arms and legs into his snowsuit, then his boots and mitts. When Alex struggled, she helped him, doing the zipper all the way up to his chin. She didn't notice when Alex set his glass of juice on the floor behind the television set. It tasted funny, so he only drank a bit. No time anyway, they were all going out to play.

Instead of heading for the snow in the front yard, Janice and Luke led the boys to the car. Strapped in, they headed down the road, the adults speaking quietly about the best spots.

They dared not go too far off the main roads in case they got the car stuck. But they needed a secondary road, hopefully one where no one would notice a mound of snow until spring.

This road might work. They'd passed one house, but Janice thought it looked deserted, with no tire tracks in or out. When they hadn't seen any motorists for twenty minutes, Luke began looking for an ideal spot.

He pulled over to the side of the road. "Okay, everybody out." He hadn't sounded this cheerful in weeks.

Matt had started to nod off, but either the cessation of the car's motion or Luke's announcement brought him back to full consciousness.

While Luke got a shovel from the trunk of the car, Janice helped her sons from their car seats, her fingers awkward with this task she'd repeated hundreds of times.

Seeing her hesitancy, Luke said, "You know this is the

best thing, don't you? It's the responsible thing to do, better for them, better for us."

"I know. It's just…"

"Are you saying you've changed your mind? What's the alternative?"

"No, no, I know it's best for them. Things are not good now and aren't going to improve."

A jovial Luke said, "Okay, boys, let's build a fort."

"Yes!" Alex got on his knees, using his hands to scoop snow as Luke put his back into shoveling a hole in the snow.

"This will be like a cave. A private hideout. Fun, eh?"

Not quite getting it, but willing to go along with anything fun, Alex got into it.

Matt bum-scooting along the snow, trying to keep up to his brother.

Soon Luke had a hole dug into the side of a sizeable snow drift. Using his booted foot, he kicked at the back of the hole, deepening the cave until it was big enough for two small boys to lay down in. Satisfied with his work, he urged the boys. "Go on, get in. See what you think."

Alex obliged, Matt scooting along behind his brother. Once inside, both boys grinned out at the adults.

Luke gave them a thumbs up.

Janice's smile wobbled and her eyes glistened with tears.

Crawling to the cave's opening, Janice stuck her head inside. She kissed Alex's forehead, then gave one to Matt. A tear fell from her eye, landing on the younger boy's cheek as he snoozed beside his brother. "You be good boys and rest here."

Catching her mood, Alex studied his mom. Was something wrong? "Mom?"

"Shoot," said Janice. "We forgot the treats. Oh, how dumb of me."

"Janice," chided Luke. "What's a man cave for the boys without treats?" Turning to the kids he said, "You stay right here. We'll go get them and be back." He picked up his shovel. "I'll just shore up the opening here a bit more so the wind can't get in. You guys rest in there all cosy. Have a little nap." He snickered. Scraping more snow with the back of his shovel, he used the new pile to almost totally block the opening to the cave.

While he worked, Janice ran to the car and back. "Here. She handed Alex a flashlight and turned it on. "You can keep this." Then she turned away, wiping her gloves across her cheeks, and trudged to the passenger seat of the car.

Tossing his shovel into the trunk, Luke got into the car and started the engine. "You okay?" he asked Janice.

She nodded; her throat too full to force out any words.

Although he hated to say the words, they needed saying. "Are you sure? It's not too late to back out of this."

"No. There's no alternative. They're better off this way. It's just, you know, hard."

Luke patted her hand as he drove away.

Janice's quiet sobs were the only noise in the car, in the world, it seemed. Everything else around them silent and still as death on this black night.

Chapter Twenty-Three

In the cave, Alex waited. And waited. Through the six-inch opening, he watched the stars twinkling in the black sky. He heard nothing, nothing except for the wind outside and the soft snoring noise Matt made. Mom said Matt snored because he was always snuffly.

Luke was right. It was cozy inside their cave, sheltered from the wind.

But where was mom? How long did it take to go get their snacks? It was hard to tell with car rides. Sometimes he napped, sometimes he didn't. But it didn't seem like they'd driven far before stopping to make this cave.

He drifted into a light doze.

It was pressure in his bladder that woke him. Mom always made him have a pee before going to sleep. She'd forgotten this time.

No, that wasn't right. He wasn't in bed, not his regular bed, or his air mattress on the floor in the kitchen. This wasn't nighttime. They were playing and Mom would be right back with their snacks. Sleep pulled him under again.

The next time Alex drifted up from slumber, his bladder said it was time. Like right now. Mom got mad when he peed the bed.

Alex sat up, bumping his head on the top of the snow cave. Ow! The snow no longer soft but coated with a light skiff of ice. Turning to look at the opening, it was hard to see outside. More snow blocked the view so all he could see was a narrow strip of inky sky.

If he didn't do something fast, he was going to pee his pants. He was a big boy, not like Matt with diapers.

He wriggled over top of Matt who didn't stir in his sleep. Using his fists, Alex pounded at the opening to make a space big enough to escape their cave. He could feel the pee pushing to get out.

Finally able to crawl out, Alex struggled in the deep snow, trying to get to his feet. Jumping from foot to foot, Alex struggled to pull down his snow pants enough to have a pee. But the straps over his shoulders wouldn't let him yank them down and the front zipper didn't extend low enough. He'd need to get his coat off first.

Several attempts to grab the zipper with his thick mitts didn't work. Putting one hand then the other into his mouth, Alex wrenched the mitts off with his teeth. His fingers were cold and didn't work properly, but he got the coat's zipper down. He let the jacket fall down his arms onto the snow.

Jiggling to try and hold it in, Alex worked one strap off his shoulder, then the second one. There. Now the snow pants zipper. Why'd it take so long? Why wouldn't his fingers work right? There were still his jeans to go, then his underwear.

Tears filled his eyes as his bladder let loose. Too soon! He still had his pants on. Oh, Mom was going to be so mad.

But it felt good, the relief from trying to hold in his pee. The warm moisture ran down his legs and into his boots.

Guilty, he looked around. Was Mom coming? Could he hide the evidence before she got here? Maybe she'd never know that he'd peed his pants.

He pulled down his snow pants but couldn't get them over his boots. Sitting down, he tugged and tugged until the boots were on the snow beside him. Then he scooted on his bum until the snow pants went down his legs and off his feet.

Bit by bit, the cold seeped into his bottom as his warmth melted the snow under him. His body shivered. Standing in his socks, he pulled down his jeans. They didn't come easily, the dampness sticking to his skin. Sitting back down in the snow, he finished shucking them off his legs.

Now it was cold. In the cave he hadn't noticed the wind. But now, in just his briefs, it felt like the wind bit at his pale legs. His fingers, numbed by the cold, couldn't hook themselves in his underwear to pull them down. Finally, his fists did the job.

Alex stood there naked, other than his shirt. Would Mom yell at him? Hit him? She hated it when he had an accident. He'd tried, really tried, but he couldn't hold it any longer. The pee just came out anyway. He hoped she wouldn't be too mad. Would the man laugh at him?

He needed to hide the wet clothes. Dropping to his knees, Alex punched at the snow with his bare fists, making the indentation bigger and bigger until it was deep enough to bury his pants and underwear. He couldn't feel his hands now, nor his knees, but they still worked.

It was cold, really cold. This wasn't fun anymore. Where was Mommy?

One sock was wet from the pee. It was hard to get off, so hard. Sitting on his bare bum in the snow hurt. First it just felt cold, like an ice cube on his tongue. Then it burned. How could something cold burn? He struggled as much as Matt would, trying to wrench that wet sock off his foot.

There. Finally. But his feet were cold, so cold. Reaching for his boots, he shoved his feet into them. That hurt, his fragile skin grating against the inside linings.

Getting back into his snow pants was harder than getting them off. His hands no longer worked right. No, it was not going to work with his boots on. They needed to come off first.

Looking down the road, there was no sign of a car. No sign of anything other than the wind and the snowflakes that were falling faster now.

How long does it take Mom to go home for the snacks and get back here?

Finally. Snow pants, jacket, and boots on. No zippers done up, though. His fingers just would not do it.

Turning in a circle, Alex surveyed his world. Now the only tracks in the snow were his own. A few dark patches showed on the road, but no tire marks. Not anymore. Nothing.

Maybe if he walked to the road, he could see the car coming. It was a lot harder walking to the road now than it had been getting off the road earlier. More snow. Colder.

But he was a big boy. He made it. Which way? Putting a

hand over his eyes, Alex tried to block the snow that hindered his vision. Looking both ways, he saw no head-lights coming toward him. No moving lights at all.

There in the distance was one light, though. It didn't move, and wasn't on the road, so that wasn't Mommy. Maybe a house. Maybe a farmhouse like Phoebe's and Jim's. That was a fun place and the grownups played with them in the snow.

Jim. Jim said don't fall asleep in the snow. Stan said that too, yelling it at Mommy. But he'd napped several times outside when he couldn't get the door open, and Mom wasn't home from work yet. That had been fine. But Jim said you'll wake up dead.

He'd never waken up dead, at least he didn't think so. But Jim and Stan were definite about not sleeping in the snow. Maybe they meant nighttime sleeping and not just short naps.

Matt was sleeping. He'd drank Mommy's sleepy juice, all of it. He seemed to like it, but it made Alex feel funny.

Mommy always told him to look after his little brother. He'd better go check on him.

Back at the cave, the entrance had almost blown in again. Digging with his hands, Alex made an opening big enough to crawl inside. Ah, it was warmer in here. No wind.

Matt wasn't snoring anymore, but he moved when Alex crawled over top of him. There wasn't enough room to sit up straight, so Alex pulled his legs to his chest and rested his head on his knees. Soon sleep overtook him.

Chapter Twenty-Four

The shaking woke him. Both his shaking and that of his little brother. Why were they shivering like this, and where was Mommy?

Alex tried lifting his head, but his mitten came with his cheek, frozen together by drool. Ow! Wrenching his hand away took some skin with it.

Still not fully awake, he checked that Mom hadn't snuck into the cave with them while they slept. Nope. And not that guy, either.

There wasn't much room in here, so maybe they were waiting outside for the boys to wake up.

It was dark in the cave, pitch black. Disoriented, Alex punched on all sides until he felt where the opening was. Or had been. It was covered in snow now, but not packed firm. His arms broke through, and he crawled out.

The movement helped slow the shivering. Standing, he looked around for Mommy. No Mommy, no man. No car, either. Just snow and wind.

Did Mommy get lost? Once he got lost in a shopping

mall. It was really scary until Mommy found him. She hugged him but got mad at the same time. If Mommy was lost, he'd hug her when she got found, and wouldn't yell at her.

Maybe he needed to look for her.

Walking to the road didn't show any sign of the car or Mommy. In the distance was a light he saw before, the one that didn't move. That was it, that was all he could see.

Was Mommy scared out here in the dark? He'd help her be brave.

Maybe she got mixed up about which on the road to go. Easy to do. She could have gone to that house to ask where the snow cave was. He'd go find her there.

He had not gone far, when he remembered Matt. Look after your little brother. Don't fall asleep in the snow or you'll wake up dead. Jim made it seem like waking up dead was a bad thing.

The snow in the ditch was deep, over the top of his boots. A misstep caused him to lift his foot right out of the boot. Boots were expensive, Mommy said. She'd be mad if he lost one and she had to replace it. Sitting down to dig around, he located the boot, emptied it of snow, and struggled it back on.

Back at the snow cave, Alex called Matt. No answer, but then Alex was used to Matt not talking. He shook his younger brother. Matt wouldn't wake up.

He needed to find Mommy. She might need his help, but he couldn't leave his brother here alone.

Grabbing hold of Matt's legs, Alex pulled as he backed up, through the opening of the cave. The wind and colder air hitting his face partially roused the toddler. He feebly fought to return to sleep, but Alex kept pulling. He dragged

Matt all the way to the road, sweating with the exertion. He lost his hat along the way.

It'd be easier on the road. Matt would wake up and work with him. Maybe he'd figure out how to walk. Together, they'd find Mommy and she would be so proud of them.

But Matt wouldn't wake up. Shaking didn't work. Neither did kicking or hollering.

Looking up and down the road, Alex tried to work out his choices. Leave Matt here and walk to the light on his own? Drag Matt back to the cave and let him sleep, then wake up dead? Or carry him to that light?

Nope, that wouldn't work. He tried, but Matt was too big, bigger than Alex even. He could get the child's shoulders off the ground, but not his legs.

Mom would want him to look after Matt. To do that, they had to stay together.

Taking hold of the back of Matt's coat, Alex dragged his brother a few steps, then a few more, before he had to rest.

The wind blew his hair into his eyes. Olivia used to cut their hair but that was a long time ago. Snow crystals stung his face and ears. He pulled the hood of his jacket over his head, but the wind took it off immediately. He hunched his shoulders up to cover his ears, but he couldn't pull Matt that way.

Was he going the right way? That light didn't get any closer.

Alex let go of his brother and sat down in the middle of the road. You're not supposed to play on the road, or you'll get run over, Mommy always said. Wish she was here now.

Matt slept on, snowflakes landing and disappearing on his face.

Get off the road. Jerry and Olivia told him that. But he couldn't pull Matt along the ditch, just couldn't.

Squinting through the snow, Alex looked for the light. Still there. He could get there faster on his own. If only Matt would wake up and walk with him. But he couldn't walk.

Look after your little brother.

Alex stumbled as he got to his feet. Facing his brother, he reached down to grasp the shoulders of Matt's coat in his fists, then, walking backward, he resumed pulling Matt toward their destination.

One foot, then the other. Over and over again. Sometimes he fell down, Matt landing on top of him. So tired. Wanted to sleep now.

His hair caked with snow, some melting and clinging to his cheeks, freezing to his scalp. Other strands dripping moisture inside his collar.

Suddenly he was on his butt in the ditch, the snow softening his landing. Hard to walk in a straight line, to stay in the middle of the road when he had to walk backwards.

How much farther?

Leaving Matt in the cushion of snow in the ditch, Alex walked on by himself. Yes, the light was getting bigger, coming from a window in a house.

Retracing his steps, Alex rolled and yanked his brother back onto the road before forcing his numb hands to grab onto Matt's shoulders and pull some more.

Stop and go. Pull, then rest. On and on into the night it went. So tempting to just drop down, cuddle up with Matt and sleep. But Mommy was lost and needed them.

Pull, pull, sit down. Pull, pull, sit down. Over and over and over again. Good boys look after their brother. Pull,

pull, rest. Pull, pull. Mommy will be so proud. Pull, pull, sit down.

Chapter Twenty-Five

Fifty-five years ago, Elliot Cleghorn built this house for his bride, Esther. Built it stick by stick with his own hands, built it to Esther's specifications. Everyone said they were crazy for putting the living room and kitchen at the back of the house, with the two bedrooms facing the road. But his Esther knew what she wanted. She wanted to look out and see the fields that provided their livelihood, the expanse of land and pasture with no one around.

They'd made a good go of things. Now, they no longer worked the land themselves, but still enjoyed the solitude of where they lived.

The television blasted out the final notes of Jeopardy's outro, waking her up. Something about TV these days put both her and Elliot right to sleep. Didn't matter what the show, or what the hour, it lulled them into snoozing.

They both had hearing aids; the kids made sure of that. But neither liked wearing them. The dang things amplified *everything* and who wanted that? When the kids came to visit, they said the TV's speakers were going to blow out because they kept the volume so high. To keep the peace during those visits, both Esther and Elliot put in their hearing aids, no matter how annoying the things were, nor how they rubbed their ears, making them sore. As delightful as it was to see the kids and grandkids, there was something relaxing when the house returned to just the two of them.

She looked affectionately at Elliot with his head back and his mouth open. A blessing of being hard-of-hearing was that Esther no longer had to put up with her husband's snoring. Oh sure, he likely snored the roof off, but it didn't prevent her from sleeping anymore.

Using both arms on the rocker to hoist herself to her feet, Esther went into the kitchen to heat up a can of tomato soup and pop some homemade bread into the toaster. Maybe she'd open a jar of pickles, the bread-and-butter ones she'd preserved last fall. Been a while since they'd sampled them.

Chapter Twenty-Six

Alex collapsed on the ground. He'd dropped his brother. He couldn't feel his hands, and they'd let go of Matt. Lifting his head, the moonlight showed his younger brother laying still in the road, near the ditch a way back.

He'd get him. He'd take care of his brother in a few minutes. He just needed to lay here a minute.

Sometime later, the cold seeping into his bones woke Alex. That, and the shivering. Turning his head and squinting, he looked toward where he thought he house lights were.

Yes, they were closer, almost there. Mommy! Maybe Mommy was inside waiting for them, and she'd be cross that it had taken them so long to get there.

Should he go and get her? She was strong and big. She could carry Matt. But no, you weren't supposed to leave your brother alone. He needed to be looked after.

Pushing to his feet, Alex winced at the feeling in his one hand. Where was his mitten? It felt like that time he'd put his hand on the burner of the stove. Boy, had he yelled and cried. But he was just a kid then, not a big boy like now. It also felt like he held an ice cube in his hand, burning and freezing at the same time. He'd have to tell Mommy about this; she'd explain it. That is, if she had time and if she wasn't too tired for all the questions he always had.

It was hard to make his hand work. Not until several tries was he able to clench the back of Matt's coat in his fists. His hands wouldn't do what they were supposed to do.

Pull, pull, sit down. Pull, pull. Soon he didn't loosen his grip on Matt's coat; it was too hard to wrap his fingers around it again if he did.

Then they were there at the house. "Mommy!" Alex yelled louder than he'd ever yelled in his life. "Mommy!"

No answer but the wind. No movement but the swirling snow blowing into drifts.

"Come on, Matt. Mom's in there." He kicked his brother. Not hard, but a kick. "Get up!"

Matt didn't move.

Looking around, Alex tried hard not to let the tears come. Mom's car wasn't here. Neither was the man's truck. Maybe Mom was still lost.

Pulling Matt was harder now that they'd left the road. There was no trail in the deep snow from the road to the door of the house.

He could do no more.

Leaving Matt to his slumber, Alex plowed his way through the drifts, struggling in thigh-high snow. Then he crawled. That way he stayed on top of the snow. Mostly. After forever and ever, he reached the porch. Using his hands and knees to climb the stairs, he yelled and beat on the door.

Mommy didn't come. No one came. He tried turning the doorknob, but his hands wouldn't work right.

Alex collapsed. Laying on his back, he felt a hint of warmth. Putting his hand to the crack under the door, warm air emitted. Not a lot, but a bit, more than he'd felt in hours and hours.

Laying there, his eyes fluttering closed, he heard his mother's voice. Look after your brother. No. He couldn't. He wasn't a big boy after all. So tired.

Look after your brother.

Rolling over, Alex looked at the deep snow between the porch and where Matt's form lay. Look after your brother.

Crawling, he left the porch and started back toward Matt.

He no longer had the strength to pull the other boy. Instead, he spread his legs and sat near Matt's head. Grasping his brother under the armpits, he pulled him towards his waist. Then Alex scooted out from beneath the sleeping child and pulled him up his thighs again. Over and over again. Pull, scoot, pull, scoot. Lay backhand pant. Pull, scoot.

The next time he lay back, his head thunked on something hard. Turning, Alex saw they were at the concrete steps of the porch.

The back of his head hurt when he bumped it. He rubbed at it and his mittened hand came away wet and dark. At least it wasn't pee. Pee made Mom the maddest. Pee and poop. He hadn't pooped his pants in a very long time.

Pulling was harder now. He had to get Matt up the steps. Leaving Matt's shoulders near the top step, Alex knelt down and heaved his brother's legs up one step, then two.

If Matt would help, it would be easier. Finally, finally, both boys were on the porch. Again, Alex tried yelling and kicking on the door. It hurt his hands too much to bang. Nothing. No Mom. Not even the man. Nobody came.

Rolling Matt over and over, he put him near the crack in the door, the one that let out some warm air. Matt had on only one boot. When had that happened? Tucking his bare hand between their bodies, Alex snuggled next to his brother and succumbed to the hand of sleep.

Chapter Twenty-Seven

"It's a cold one out tonight," said Elliot Cleghorn. "Just listen to that wind."

Esther set the last of the cleaned dishes to dry in the rack by the sink. The kids had insisted on installing a dishwasher, but what was the point in that? With just the two of them, how many dishes did they use? It was faster for her to wash them herself, than to load and unload the blasted machine.

Elliot banked the embers in the fireplace, and set the spark arrester screen in place, same as he did every winter night before bed.

Esther resettled the blanket they used as a draft catcher by the front door. Darned door had warped and now let in a chilly breeze. Next time the kids came home, she'd ask them to look at it. Elliot's hands were no longer up to the woodworking and repairs he used to take pride in.

The couple retired for the evening, although their sleep no longer looked like it had once upon a time. Esther remembered fondly the days when they took sleep for granted. You went to bed. You fell asleep immediately. You woke up seven or eight hours later refreshed.

Now, they might go to bed with good intentions. Then their bladders demanded attention. How had they ever held their water for a full eight hours? Now it seemed like every few hours one of them had to get up to pee. Falling back asleep immediately rarely happened, either. Sometimes one of them would turn on the TV, that sleep aid guaranteed to knock them out. Sometimes one of them would wake up early in the morning, too early, since they no longer had chickens or cattle to feed. Still, such was life. She couldn't complain.

The drive home was silent. Luke kept glancing at Janice but said nothing. He wasn't stupid.

Janice's head rested against the passenger side window, her eyes closed. He'd already offered to turn around, and she'd bitten his head off. So, he'd let her handle this her way. He wasn't heartless, after all. He knew this was tough on her. Just because it was the right thing to do didn't make it easy. He got that.

When he turned into their driveway and switched off the engine, Janice still didn't move. Luke exited the car and went to the other side of the car to open the passenger door. With one hand of her arm, he gently helped his girlfriend out of the vehicle, then led her through the path in the snow to the front door. "Tomorrow I'll shovel this," he offered. "Make it easier to walk."

No response.

Well, he'd tried.

Once inside, he sat Janice on the couch. Kneeling, he removed her boots for her. Don't let anyone say he didn't know how to be a gentleman. "Want something to drink? Maybe a shot of bourbon?" He knew *he* could sure use one.

Janice shook her head.

Maybe he'd make her one anyway. Heat it up with some water and butter and brown sugar, like a toddy. It was a cold night and they'd been out in the snow. Yeah, that was a good idea. "Sit tight. I've got something special for you." He'd even add a sprinkle of cinnamon on top. He knew how to look after a woman.

It didn't take long to make with the help of the microwave. Looked and smelled so good, he made himself one, too. "Here," he said as he wrapped Janice's fingers around the warm mug. "It's good for what ails ya." When she made no motion to avail herself of his offering, he tilted the mug toward her mouth, encouraging her to sip.

Reflexively, Janice allowed some of the hot liquid to enter her mouth. Swallowing, she gave a crest of a smile, her lips barely tilting upward at the corners. It was the best she could do. Luke was trying, she could see that. He really was an all-right guy. She drank some more, until the drink was half gone.

Luke moved to sit beside her on the couch, his arm circling her shoulders, pulling her close.

For a while, Janice rested there, taking comfort in this man. He really did care for her. What little time they had together would be good.

Reflexively, her hand rose to her breast. No, she told herself. Quit fiddling with it. No point in squishing out those cancer cells, making them migrate all over her body. Tears spilled from her eyes.

Just how much time did she have? What would the end be like? Would it hurt? Of course, it would hurt. There would be pain and lots of it. If she was in hospital, they'd be able to douse her up to dull the pain. But she had no money for medical care. What if she had to die at home in agony? Maybe she should have stayed with Alex and Matt, peacefully drifting off to sleep, then knowing no more. By the time this disease reeked its havoc, it would be summer with no chance of slipping out of this world quietly in the snow. Had she screwed up?

Luke gathered her closer. Let her cry it out. That's what women did, wasn't it? This was a traumatic night for her, but they'd get past it.

Chapter Twenty-Eight

Something bothered Esther as she lay there in bed. What was it? As her brain cells started getting their act together, the sleep haze receded, and she remembered. Yes! Today was the day her grandkids were coming.

So much to do. The kids might not care if her house was spotless, but she did. There was a time when she could whip through the housework, having everything tiptop in no time. Now, not so much. That same cleaning had to be carefully spread over several days. Well, not much left to do before company arrived.

She climbed out of bed carefully, partly so as not to awaken Eliot, partly to give her joints time to adjust to what was expected of them. The kids were always warning her about not falling and breaking a hip.

That reminded her of the first chore of the day. It had snowed a lot since either of them had left the house. Why bother when they had everything they needed right here? But with the kids coming, she needed to get the porch and steps shovelled off. Eliot would do the walk when he got up. It's how they'd always divided this job.

Slipping into the bathroom, Esther got dressed. A long-time habit, she kept her next day's clothes in there so she could get ready to meet the day without waking Eliot. Poor man. He slept even worse than she did these days, so he needed his rest.

In the kitchen freshly brewed coffee awaited her. At first when the kids bought her an automatic coffee maker with a timer, she'd scoffed. But it truly was a blessing to set things up the night before, then wake up to the aroma of her caffeinated beverage all ready and waiting for her.

She sat at the kitchen table, sipping from her favorite mug, enjoying the view of the snow-swept fields, and doing her daily crossword puzzle. Good to keep the mind in shape. She prided herself on doing the hard ones, not leaving her spot at the table until every box was filled in correctly.

Done. Satisfied that her brain was still up to snuff, Esther rinsed her cup at the kitchen sink. Using the bench by the front door, she sat to put on her winter boots. From the hooks on the wall, she got her coat. Unlike Eliot, who constantly had to search for everything, Esther's gloves were right in the pocket of her coat where she'd left them. Grabbing the broom and shovel they kept by the door, she used her foot to shove back the draft catcher, then pulled open the front door.

The screen door opened outwards. Sometimes, especially in winter, it stuck a bit. She gave it a push with her hip, the usual strategy that worked. But today the door only moved an inch or so. Putting more oomph into it, she shoved harder with her hip, that same one the kids told her to be careful with. Well, she was not strong enough to push open the door with her arthritic hands, but her ample bottom gave some heft to her hip thrust. Still, it didn't work. The door only opened a hand's width.

Had it snowed that much that she was working against a drift? Glancing through the glass, Esther looked down. Yeah, there was a mound of snow inconsiderately piled against the door. She blew out a breath. Did this mean she had to go out the back door and trudge all around the house in order to shovel off the porch? Lifting your feet through knee-high snow was hard on old bones.

Maybe she'd have another cup of coffee first.

A glance at her watch told her that she needed to get a move on if she wanted to get all her tasks finished before the kids arrived.

How hard could the snow be? She'd shoved it a few inches. If she could get the door even a foot open, it would be enough for her to squeeze through, then she could attack the stubborn snow.

Repeated hip action gained her another inch. Slow going. Maybe she could slip her hand through the crack and push some of the snow away.

Using the shovel and the bench for balance, Esther lowered herself until she was on her hands and knees. Too bad she didn't have on the knee pads she wore when gardening in the summer.

Pushing her left hand through the door's opening, she brushed away snow as best she could, making some progress. Shifting her position to give her more reach, the back of Esther's hand touched something different, something with less give than packed snow. Frowning, she tried again, turning her palm up this time. Her fingers found material. Quickly, she dug, uncovering more and more blue cloth. The cloth took form. She reached higher and her fingers found something hard and round. Good Lord! Was that hair?

Pushing with all her might, heedless of her hips, Esther shoved and shoved. Finally, she could squeeze her skinny, old self through the opening. Bending down in just her polyester pants, she dug with her bare hands, cursing the arthritis that robbed her of full control over her fingers. Cleaning away white stuff, her hands met strands of soft hair, fine hair. Then she found the face. A child's face, innocent in slumber. Or death. It was hard to tell from the cold skin.

Esther was no stranger to life and death, having farmed over almost six decades, tending to livestock through good times and bad. She tried for a pulse along the side of his neck, but her frozen fingers didn't give a reliable report. Steeling herself, she held a finger under the child's nose. Was there a faint exhalation of air?

Burying her hands underneath the child, she tried to free him from the snow, then lift him. She got his body to her thighs, but her strength gave out, despite her will. Cursing old age, she tried comforting the still form. "I'll be right back. Elliot will carry you inside. You'll be fine."

"Elliot," she screamed. "Elliot, get out here!"

With the snows soaking into her pants, she waited. No response. That darned man. He couldn't hear a thing above his own snoring. Bracing herself with one hand against the door frame, Esther brought herself to her knees, then her feet. She'd have to go get Elliot.

Despite her desperation for speed, her old bones defied her. Her knees just would not bend and straighten as they should, supporting her weight. When her left one collapsed beneath her, she lay on her side to wiggle through the partially opened door, then half-crawled, half-dragged herself into the bedroom. Using the nightstand and bed as leverage, she pulled herself erect, pummelling Elliot's shoulders.

"What, what?" He sputtered awake. "Lord love a duck, woman, what are you beating me for?"

"There's a child on our steps. He looks frozen, but I think he's alive. I can't get him inside."

A lifetime spent responding to the needs of his livestock and his crops had Elliot's mind on alert instantly. His body not so much. But he tried. Pushing his feet into the tattered, open-backed slippers the kids said would be the death of him, Elliot made it to the front door.

"Don't push too hard, you might hurt the child," warned Esther.

"How do you expect me to get to him if I don't open the door?" Complaining under his breath about women who needed to organize everything, he heaved on the door, then was outside, the wind flapping the wide leggings of his flannelette pajamas. Brushing off snow, he uncovered the form of a child, a small one. Maybe not even in school yet. How had a kid come to be on their doorstep?

Looking around, he searched for a car. Maybe a family had gotten in trouble and this child came to them for help. But there was no car. No one at all, except this poor youngster.

Carefully, Elliot wrapped him in his arms, pulling him to his chest. Now what? Once upon a time, this was a common posture for Elliot, rising with a newborn calf in his arms, one who needed tending to. Back then, his knees didn't give it a thought, rising as they should, taking their burden without protest.

But Esther was there. Esther understood. With her help,

he got to his feet, ready to take the precious burden inside, when Esther shrieked.

Now, his Esther had seen a lot in her day. He didn't know how many breech births she'd attended, always helping, never shying from the dirty or unpleasant aspects of farm life. Never had he heard her shriek.

"Elliot! There's another one!" Stark terror on her face as she pointed.

What they'd thought was simply more of the snow drift, was another snow-covered form.

While Esther frantically uncovered the second body, Elliot made his way into the house, laying the child on the bed he and his wife recently vacated. Brushing the child's hair from his face, Elliot told the still form, "I'll be right back with your brother or sister." How many of them were out there?

Chapter Twenty-Nine

Many a calf had been born in a blizzard. They'd found them and nursed them through. Lost a few, sure, but not many.

It was different with human young though.

Elliot could see when the horror receded from his wife's mind and her instincts took over. She removed the boys' damp and snowy clothing. Why was the one boy naked under his snowsuit? They snuggled the kids under layers of homemade quilts and comforters. Gently she blew on their hands and feet. With calves, and lambs, they rubbed them with soft cloths. Was it the same with frostbitten children? Looking at the blisters on the one boy's foot and the one's hand, they thought not. Instead, they wrapped those limbs in clean towels.

With the one child, she feared it was in vain. She couldn't tell if he was alive or dead. Elliot looked up at her from where he worked trying to warm up the boy's feet. They'd found the child with one boot on, but the other foot had been bare of either boot or sock. Elliot rapped on the foot. No sign the child felt a thing, but to Elliot, it felt like tapping a block of wood.

It was one thing to do what they thought best when rescuing animals. Afraid of doing more harm than good, Esther signalled to Elliot to stop. They covered the boys and went into the hall to confer.

Esther phoned 911, reporting what they'd found on their doorstep. So far, the boys were unresponsive, and they needed help fast. The 911 operator asked if there were signs of life in the children. In one, yes; they just weren't sure about the other one.

Hanging up, they went back to their vigil over the boys. There was a resemblance, definitely, so they were probably brothers, but they were similar in size. Twins, maybe?

The boy Esther found first stirred under the blankets. Instantly, Esther was by his side, kneeling beside the bed, stroking his hair. "We're here, honey. You're safe now."

He didn't open his eyes but said one word. "Mommy?"

Good Lord in Heaven. Was there more of them out there?

While Esther made another call to 911 to alert them of the possible presence of someone else outside in the snow, Elliot geared up to search the deep snow in the yard.

"Will the snowshoes help?" Esther asked.

Maybe. Blasted things. They worked well once on, and would make trudging around the yard easier, but that meant he had to bend over to buckle them on. Damn.

When you live in a rural area, help doesn't arrive in minutes. It was more like half an hour, which wasn't bad, considering the conditions.

The EMTs arrived puffing with the exertion of toting

their equipment and gurneys through the deep snow. They found vital signs in both children, although it was fainter in the one.

Packing the boys' extremities in sterile bandages, then wrapping their bodies in sheets and blankets, the EMTs loaded the children onto gurneys and began the arduous trip to their ambulance in the snow. Being young and fit, they made the trip faster than Elliot in his snowshoes. With sirens flashing, they left for the hospital in Ely, over half an hour away.

In the meantime, troopers convinced Elliot to go back into the house as they continued to search the property for signs of any other bodies.

Esther kept the coffee pot full and the sandwiches flowing to the officials who spent the day in the cold, searching.

Shortly before noon, an SUV pulled up, which was immediately surrounded by officers of the law. Elliot hustled into his coat and boots to assure those with badges that this was his son and grandkids, come for a scheduled visit. They knew nothing about the boys they'd found half-frozen on their doorstep.

Neither the human nor the canine searchers found any signs of people on the farm. But the dogs followed the children's trail down the road to a snowbank. Digging found no evidence of more people alive or otherwise, just a pair of buried jeans.

The police bagged the boys' clothes. The dogs found the missing mitt, boot, and sock along the trail to the snowbank. Nothing but generic tags on the apparel, no names. No identifiers at all.

Canvassing neighbors brought no clues. No one was missing two small children or had seen any around.

No calls to police stations reported missing boys. No sign of who they belonged to.

Chapter Thirty

By the next morning, Alex roused enough to respond to questions. Social workers led the questioning but were just as frustrated as the police at trying to get useful information out of a four-year-old.

They learned a few facts. Their names were Alex and Matt, although sometimes Alex slipped and said Matteo. He explained that you're supposed to say Matt here, but sometimes when you went somewhere else, you said Matteo.

Alex was sure he was four, or at least that's how many fingers he held up in response to being asked his age. He said his brother was two, but something seemed off with that as the two boys were about the same size.

His mother's name was Mommy. She lived with "that guy". They came here after a long drive. They met some nice men once who played with them in the snow. *That* got the cops attention.

These were small towns in rural areas. Everyone knew everyone, or at least about them. How did two little boys get here without anyone noticing?

After another day of no luck identifying the boys, a Judge granted permission for their pictures to be aired publicly.

At their farmhouse, Phoebe and Jim watched the Fargo news after supper, chatting about their grandchildren, only half-paying attention to the television. Entering the living room after refreshing his cup of coffee, their son, Stan halted and stared. "Mom, aren't those the kids we rescued last month?"

Three sets of eyes turned to the TV screen. "...found nearly frozen to death on the front steps of an elderly couple's farmhouse...both now in stable condition...some amputation might be required. If anyone has information on their identity, please call...".

Stan had his cell phone out. "What were their names? Did we ever get last names?"

"Janice was the mom." Phoebe and Jim looked at each other. Neither knew the surname.

"Embarrass, Minnesota. That's where they were going," remembered Jim.

"There can't be too many new people with two boys in a town that size." Stan went into the hall to talk to the authorities. "And didn't Janice call the guy she heading to Luke?"

"Shit!" Luke spewed out his beer. "Janice, get out here. Those brats are on TV."

Janice stood by Luke's recliner, staring at the TV, at the images of her two boys staring back at her.

"They don't look dead." Luke listened to the reporter. "Can you believe it? Someone found them. Now they're in the hospital."

Relief mixed with regret filled Janice. The boys were okay, but the plan hadn't worked.

"Okay, keep calm," said Luke. "It's no problem. They don't know who the kids belong to. The brat only gave their first names and has no idea where we live. They could be anybody's kids."

They could be, but they weren't, thought Janice. She tried to do the right thing by them, and not leave them motherless at the hands of the system. Now, it looked like they'd be in the system anyway.

She ignored Luke as he swore away about damned kids always ruining everything.

She weighed the options. If she came forward as their mother, she'd get in trouble. There had to be some sort of law against leaving your kids in a snowbank. If she got thrown in jail, the boys would still be wards of the state, and part of the system. No matter what, that's how they'd end up.

But for Janice, there was a choice. No point in her spending the rest of her life behind bars, when it wouldn't do the boys any good anyway.

The next day the town buzzed with talk of the images on the news last night. Can you imagine? How could two little boys get lost in the snow? Where were their parents? They must be frantic.

At the diner, Nancy said, "They must be around the same age as your two. Their poor mother. Makes you want to hold yours tight, doesn't it?"

Janice said all the right things and kept her head down. Luke said it was fine. No one knew who the kids belonged to, and Alex wasn't able to give any information other than his first name and that of his brother. According to the news report, the child said they lived with Mommy and that man.

She'd just gotten her monthlies and was almost out of supplies. During her break, Janice slipped out to the pharmacy to get what she needed. Was it her imagination, or did the pharmacist watch her more closely than usual?

Her seven o'clock shift began as normal the next day, some of the gossip about the lost boys was replaced by news about the faulty heat lamp that started a fire in the Larson's hen house.

Shortly after, officials descended on the little town armed with photos of the two boys and questions. They had the town. They had the names Janice and Luke. In a town of fewer than a thousand people, it didn't take long to narrow things down.

Janice worked only about ninety minutes of her shift before she was asked to accompany the police for questioning. The three men surrounding made it less a request than an order. Nancy and the customers in the diner watched appalled and enthralled as Janice was arrested under suspicion of child endangerment.

Less than half an hour later, Luke found himself in the back of a squad car under similar charges. Those were just the preliminary ones, he was told, despite protesting his innocence. They weren't his kids. He knew nothing about what the mother had done with them.

Chapter Thirty-One

Janice caved. It was that woman cop, acting all sympathetic about how tough it was raising kids, especially as a single mom, then trying to date and have a relationship. She pretended she was all on Janice's side, even patting her hand.

"You want the best for your boys, I know you do," she said.

Janice nodded. What else could she do?

"See, here's the thing. We need to find a home for Luke and Matt, a good home. Do you have any relatives who would take them?"

This time Janice shook her head. "We have no family in this country."

"Were the boys born here?"

"No, in Mexico."

"Then they're Mexican citizens." She wrote something in her notebook and looked up at the window in one wall. "Is there anyone here in Minnesota who would take in your sons?"

No, they didn't know anyone here, other than her boss and Luke's. Neither were exactly friends. Janice thought of Olivia and Jerry. They might, but they were half a country away. Besides, they were old, and struggled to make ends meet for themselves.

"Is there no one else you can think of?"

Wait. What about the people who helped them when her car seized? Phoebe and Jim. Yeah, they were old, too, but their sons weren't, and the sons had played with the boys. They'd all been nice to the kids, even though they were virtual strangers.

"There was one family..." Sheesh. Janice realized she didn't even know their last name.

"Anything you can think of will help the boys," said the officer. "And it could help your case, as well. You know, show your cooperation and concern about the kids' welfare."

Was there a note of sarcasm in the woman's voice? Never mind. She had too much else to think about. "I can't remember their surname, but they lived on a farm. They were good people - Phoebe and Jim. Their sons were Stan and Greg, adults themselves, and Greg had a family of his own."

Taking notes, the office asked, "Where in Minnesota was this?"

"No, I don't think we'd reached Minnesota yet. It was the other side of Fargo, North Dakota, but not too far from the city. They were really nice, rescuing us when my car broke down, looking after the boys so I could sleep in, giving us winter clothes, playing with the kids." She used the one hand that wasn't chained to the chair to take a sip of the tepid coffee they'd given her. "Oh yeah. And they loaned me their car."

"They did?" Skepticism in her voice.

"Yes. They were wonderful about it. Said they weren't using it, and they'd lend it to me until I got to Embarrass, then Luke and I could return it to them."

"Really. And when was this?"

Time was a fluid thing for Janice. It easily got away on her. "Not sure. A while back. Before I started at the diner. Nancy would be able to tell you when I started working for her."

"I'll be sure to ask her." She paused to write for a while, then looked up. "What makes you think these people would take in your children?"

"Well, they were nice. Seemed like good people."

"Good people. Good enough that you took their car and didn't return it?"

"No, it's not like that. The car was a loan. I meant to return it but haven't had a chance yet. I've got a job and kids, don't you understand?"

"Yes. I think I understand what's going on."

"Good."

The woman raised an eyebrow, but bit off what she was going to say. "So, this car. Is it registered in your name?"

Janice had given no thought at all to the vehicle's registration. Or insurance. Could she get in trouble for this?

The officer continued. "Do you think the car is registered in the name of the actual owners?"

Janice shrugged. "That's a good guess."

"Okay." She raised her eyes to the window again. "We'll have some people trace it, and try to contact these people."

"Thanks. I don't want my boys becoming part of the system. Phoebe and Jim will look after them. They have to, or all this would have been for nothing."

Chapter Thirty-Two

It hurt. Everything hurt, but most of all his hand and his throat and his head and when he tried to pee. Maybe his stomach, too. They had his hand all wrapped up with this thick, white stuff and taped to a board. Sometimes that felt okay, but then the mean ladies would come and undo it all and put goop on his hand. They said it was to make it better, but it made it hurt more.

In the bed beside him, Matt slept. He had his hands bandaged, but not a big, fat one like Alex. More like Alex's other hand. But Matt's one foot was all wrapped up. He screamed and fought the people when they'd come to do things to it. The first few times it happened, Alex struggled to climb out of bed to help his brother, but it was hard. They had him in a cage, sort of like when Matt was a baby and slept in a little bed with bars on the sides.

The people tried to make Matt stand on his hurt foot. They wanted him to walk. Alex kept telling them Matt didn't walk, but they never listened.

If Mommy was here, she'd tell them. But Mommy never

came. Was she still lost? She wouldn't know that he'd looked after his brother.

"As usual, sons, we thank you for your thoughtful, if loud, input." Jim tried to bring this family meeting to a close.

"No way! No way, Dad, are you taking in those kids. You're old! Do you know how much energy boys that age take?"

"Oh, we have an idea, son. We raised you and your brother." Phoebe and Jim shared a smile.

"But that was ages ago. Aggie and I know that you love our kids but are tired after babysitting for a day, glad when we take them home."

This time the older couple's glance together held a tinge of guilt.

"These kids have no option, other than to be split up into different foster homes. After what they've been through, they deserve better."

"Yeah, they deserve better than a mother who'd steal our car, then abandon her kids to die in the cold. But that's not *our* problem, not *your* problem."

Phoebe patted her son's hand. "Sometimes when you see an opportunity to do a little good in the world, you need to take it." She stood up, the signal that this discussion reached its end. "Besides the boys will be in the hospital for some time yet, with Alex losing two fingers and that poor Matt having half his foot amputated."

Governments don't work fast, especially when crossing jurisdictions. You might think it a simple thing to get two small boys across state lines to a home where they were wanted.

Such was not the case.

Out of compassion, the hospital kept Alex a few extra days, but beds cost money and it was time. He moved into a temporary foster home that already held six other children of various ages.

Matt's foot took longer to heal, with more of it needing to be cut away. The Minnesota Department of Human Services eventually received the child's medical records from California thanks to information from the North Dakota family who had offered the mom and boys hospitality for a night. They now had an explanation for Matt's lack of talking or walking. Not trauma-related as they'd expected, but a developmental delay.

Matt was sent to a medical foster home upon release from hospital.

It took almost another month before the Minnesota and North Dakota departments worked out who was paying and who'd take responsibility for the boys. But eventually, Jim and Phoebe receive the okay. Bonus - they could also get back their car that had remained in the police impound since Janice's arrest.

Stan drove his parents from their home to Minnesota. It was a long, long five hours, with Stan giving it his all to convince his parents of the folly of taking in these boys. He came at it from every angle he could think of, all the arguments Greg and his wife Aggie had added as well. Phoebe and Jim were old. They had the farm work to do, with no time to tend to kids all day. And these weren't just any kids, but traumatized ones.

"How are you going to explain to the kids that their mother tried to kill them?"

"We won't." Phoebe and Jim had already discussed this. "Not our place. Besides, we don't know for sure that's what happened. The trial hasn't even begun."

"Riiiight." Stan had already shared his views of that woman. "Don't you think they'll ask you, want to talk about what happened?"

"There are professionals for that. Our role is to love them and make them feel safe and secure."

Jim added, "We'll give them sanctuary. When you see a chance to do good in this world, you do what you have to do."

It felt weird. Riding in Mommy's car, but no Mommy. Instead, Jim drove. Matt fell asleep soon after they got underway. Alex hadn't seen Phoebe or Jim give him sleepy juice, and they didn't offer him any.

No one talked about Mommy. Phoebe said she wouldn't be joining them on the farm. It had been a long time since he'd seen Mommy, even though people told him she wasn't lost.

Stan and Greg didn't play with them; they didn't seem so friendly anymore. But they didn't yell like Luke did.

They settled into life at Jim's and Phoebe's farm. Jim tried to hang around the house, helping Phoebe when Matt needed to be carried.

One morning, Jim worked in the barn while Phoebe gave Matt a bath, after a really stinky diaper change. Lifting him out of the tub, Phoebe's foot slipped on the mat, sending both her and Matt tumbling to the floor. Matt howled, holding his foot. Phoebe shrieked, then stayed down. Tears spilled down her cheeks.

"Alex. You need to go get help. I'm hurt."

How?

"Put on your coat and boots and go to the barn to get Jim."

The barn. He wasn't supposed to go in there by himself. He wasn't supposed to go outside by himself at all. It was cold out there, and lots of snow. But Phoebe was crying. She wasn't getting up.

"Hurry now. Be a big boy and get help."

A big van came with flashing lights. Two men in uniforms ran into the house. They lifted Phoebe onto one low bed with wheels, and Matt on another, and drove away with them, Jim following in his truck.

Stan put Alex in the car and drove him to Greg's and Aggie's house.

Chapter Thirty-Three

She doesn't like me, Alex thought. She doesn't yell like that man Luke did, but she doesn't want me here.

Her boy doesn't want me touching his toys. That's all right. I don't need toys.

The girl is just a baby, crawling around. She cried while her mom was in the bathroom. He tried to help by changing her diaper. Aggie came in while he was doing it and got mad. She snatched up the baby and told him to get out of the room.

Didn't she know that he was a big boy, that he knew how to change a diaper? He'd done it lots for Matt.

Now Aggie and Greg talked to each other in loud whispers, the kind where they thought kids couldn't hear.

"What are we supposed to do with him?"

Greg ran his hands through his hair. "Beats me. Stan and I told Mom and Dad it was a bad idea to take in these kids."

"Well, they did, and it looks like we're stuck with them

now. Or at least one of them," said Aggie. "Where's he supposed to sleep? It's not like we have an extra bedroom, or even an extra bed."

Was that the problem? Where he'd sleep? Making himself as small as possible, Alex crept into the bathroom. Tugging, he pulled two towels onto the floor. Taking them with him into the kitchen, he crawled under the table, spreading out the towels as best he could into a bed, the way he had at that Luke man's house. Maybe they'd get him an air mattress like Mommy did.

Noticing movement beneath the kitchen table, Aggie whirled. "What are you *doing*?" She glared at Greg. "Just what I need, another mess to clean up. *You* deal with him. I've had it." She did that stomping thing with her feet as she left, the way Mommy did when it was best to keep out of her way. A few seconds later, a bedroom door slammed.

Phoebe was in hospital. She broke her hip. She needed surgery. Surgery hurt. Surgery cut off two of his fingers. Now they were short, like a baby's, but with no fingernails. Surgery cut off half of Matt's foot, and now they were doing more surgery on it. Would they cut off the rest of his brother's foot?

Alex hoped surgery wouldn't hurt Phoebe like it hurt him. Were they cutting off her hip? Greg and Aggie and Stan talked about Phoebe being unable to walk. They moved her stuff from the upstairs bedroom down into the one he and Matt shared. Now Alex's clothes were in a box in the corner of Aggie and Greg's living room. He didn't know where Matt's things were, but they said Matt was in hospital like Phoebe.

Two days later, Greg took Alex to the hospital. He didn't say much on the drive, other than "My mother wants to talk to you."

The glass doors slid open with a whoosh. So many people. Don't get lost. With difficulty, Alex tried matching his strides to Greg's. Taking two at a time kept him just a few steps behind, requiring a couple skips to keep up.

They got on a crowded elevator. A woman stepped on his toe with her pointy heel. She didn't say sorry. Too bad it hadn't been Matt's foot she trod on because he didn't have any foot in that spot anymore.

As the elevator doors opened, the smells of the place entered the little box they were in. Those were smells of hurt, of strangers fussing over him, jabbing him, moving his around when he just wanted to be left alone. Machines beeping, lies when they said, "…you'll feel a little poke…", Matt crying in the bed next to him.

Greg's hand on his upper arm pulled him down the hall. "Hey, Mom." The man leaned over and kissed Phoebe on the cheek. "Here he is, as you requested." He stepped away, motioning Alex to the side of the bed.

Frozen, images of hospital beds and pain fast-forwarding through his brain, Alex didn't move until Greg's shove pushed him to Phoebe's side.

Phoebe looked different. Smaller. Her hair was every which way. She had one of the pokey things sticking out from the back of her hand. Machines beeped away, wires running from Phoebe to them.

She put her hand on top of his head, a hand with the pokey thing taped to it. Could it fall out of her hand and jab into him? Did it hurt her?

"Alex, I have something to tell you," said Phoebe. "We wanted you boys to have a home with us."

Yeah, they did. It was good. Always food and no one yelled.

"When I fell, I broke my hip. It's a bad break and will take a long time to heal. That means I can't lift Matt."

"Jim can. He's big and strong. Or Greg or Stan. I can help."

Phoebe smiled, but her eyes were sad. Maybe she hurt. "I'm sorry, but we can't keep you boys anymore."

Can't? Where would they go? "Mommy?"

Phoebe shook her head. "No, your mother isn't able to look after your either."

Then what? He and Matt had spent one night outside all by themselves, and that had been bad. He's tried to be a good big brother, but he wasn't big enough to look after him all by himself. "Will we stay with Greg and Aggie?"

"No, they don't have enough room. You're going to a foster home. The social worker will pick you up this afternoon."

"What's a foster home?"

"It's a family like ours, who takes in children who need a home."

"Matt, too." A statement, not a question.

Phoebe and Greg exchanged looks. "I'm not sure. Matt's still in hospital. The social worker will sort it out and let you know."

"Mommy?"

"No, your mommy won't be coming. She made mistakes and must pay for them in jail."

He tried, he really tried to be a big boy. But it was all too much, all too scary. Greg and Aggie didn't want them. Phoebe and Jim didn't want them anymore. And Mommy? Couldn't she say sorry for the mistake and come for them?

Sinking to the floor, Alex scrunched himself into the

smallest ball possible and all the pent-up sobs stormed out in a torrent.

The social worker waited in the visitor's section of the woman's jail, conflicted about this meeting. Technically, the state now had custody of the boys, but the placement had broken down.

Janice entered. A guard held one of her handcuffed arms and guided her to a chair across the table from the social worker.

"I have some bad news for you. The placement for your sons has broken down. The foster mother is in hospital. She's no longer able to care for the boys." She waited for a reaction. When none came, she continued. "Is there anyone else you know who would take your children?"

See? This is what happened when plans didn't work out. She'd tried to do what was best for her kids and now this. What did they expect her to do? They'd stuck her in this place. She couldn't exactly look after the kids herself, could she? And yet, here they were, coming to her to solve the problem for them.

The social worker continued. "We can, of course, find new homes for them. But it's best for kids if they can be with a relative or close friend of the family."

Relative. There was only one, really. "There's my mother, but she's not here. She lives in Rosarito, Mexico."

Flipping through her file, the social worker checked. "The boys are Mexican citizens, right?"

"Yeah, they were born there."

"Good. This might work out then. How can we get in touch with your mother?"

Janice let the thoughts race through her mind, sorting out the options. "First, can I ask you a question?"

The social worker nodded.

"Since I'm in jail, it's not like I can just go see a doctor. I have a medical condition and need treatment. Can you get that for me?"

"Certainly. I'll let the warden know."

Janice smiled for the first time since her arrest. Maybe things happened for a reason. She gave Elena's address and phone number, at least the last number she remembered. It had been a few years since she'd used it.

Abuelita Elena was less than thrilled. She'd raised her kids, mostly on her own. Why couldn't Juana do the same for her own kids?

But no, Juana had screwed up, as she was wont to do. Royally this time, landing her ass in jail. Now she expected Elena to clean up after her, taking on two grandsons.

Feeding kids cost money. She'd said as much to the woman on the phone. Since the boys were currently wards of the state of Minnesota, there was some money involved. Not a ton of it, but they'd provide support for the boys for a period of twelve months.

Twelve months. Anything could happen in that amount of time. Maybe Juana would get her act together and come get her kids by then.

"For a full twelve months?" Best check about these things. "No matter what?"

"That's what the contract will stipulate," was the answer.

Plus, they'd fly her up to Minnesota to collect the boys,

then fly the three of them back home again. She'd heard about snow, but never seen it. She'd never been on a jet plane.

This might be okay.

Part II

Part II

Chapter Thirty-Four

Present Day

It had been a little over two years since Natalie came to live with her father, her real father, not the fake one she'd known all her life.

Finding out that Alejandro was her birth father changed her world. No longer did she feel alone. *This* man understood her, not like the adoptive parents who raised her. They'd always looked at her like a bug under a microscope. Oh, they tried, she knew that, but there were just too many differences for it to have worked. They provided for her, sure, and loved her the best they could, but it was forced. They did it because they were supposed to, it was expected of them, but there had never been a real connection.

But with Alejandro, it was different. She was enough. There was no unstated pressure to conform, to fit in with what they wanted her to be. He accepted her as she was. Without saying anything, without the constant pressure to explain why, he got her. Refreshing. She wasn't a freak; there was someone just like her.

He didn't try to make her into something she wasn't, not like her parents, teachers and every other adult she'd ever met had tried to do.

Life with Alejandro was good.

The frustration over all those things her adoptive parents denied her under the pretext there wasn't enough money. Gone, all of it. With Alejandro, she could have whatever she wanted. Life with him was more like what she deserved.

He indulged her; a girl had to like that. There was only one area where they butted heads. Well, maybe two.

Once, that annoying cat had lurked around her feet, trying to trip her. She'd tried moving the thing away with the side of her foot. Alejandro noticed and lit into her – the only time he'd raised his voice to her. Sheesh. She didn't actually *kick* the thing…

The other contentious area had been school. He wouldn't budge on that.

What use was school anyway? The kids hated her and so did the teachers. Always on her case, always trying to make her fit in, to do meaningless stuff. None of it related to real life, not to *her* life. She got along just fine without school.

But Alejandro insisted. He'd given her two weeks to settle in and make up her mind. Did she want to attend the local public school, a private school or take classes online? Those were the three options, nothing else.

She waited right until the fourteenth day, still mostly believing he'd drop it, but he didn't. She chose right then, or he chose for her.

Online seemed the least intrusive option. No annoying

peers, no teacher looking over her shoulder, sending her to the office, or generally trying to boss her around. Plus, who knew what was going on with an online class? Just some faceless human out in cyberspace, or maybe even some robot.

Problem was, Alejandro knew. The first month, he let her do her own thing. Then the monthly report came, letting the guardian know the work that had been accomplished, plus the grades.

For the first time ever, Alejandro verged on losing his patience with her. Yeah, she'd been used to that with her parents and every teacher she'd ever met, but not with Alejandro.

"What do I need school for, anyway? It's pointless."

"No, it's not pointless. It's a means to an end. If you don't finish high school and get decent grades, you won't get into college."

"So? Who said I wanted to go to any college anyway?"

"*I* do. And it matters not if you want to go to college or not, you are going, and you will do well."

"People go to college so they can get a good job. That's what Howard and Barbara used to tell me. It doesn't matter now that I'm with you. You have enough money. I don't need to worry about a job."

He'd just looked. Usually Alejandro doted on her, regarding her with approval and acceptance. She wasn't used to that annoyed stance her parents used to take - annoyed and disappointed in her. And frustrated.

Alejandro didn't seem frustrated. Just resolute.

So, fine. She'd knuckled down and done the stupid work. All of it. Maybe not well, but well enough to meet the minimum requirements Alejandro set.

But it was over now. She'd finished grade 12. She'd never get back all those wasted hours, but at least now she could begin living her life.

Except, no. Alejandro had other plans. "You're not sitting on your duff. You're going to work and you're going to college."

Chapter Thirty-Five

Natalie was not giving up.

"What do I need college for? You have more money than God. We don't need the little bit I could bring in. Besides, I could have a job without going to college."

"True. And you will work. For me."

Alejandro traveled lots. That would be fun. "Okay. I'll work for you. What will I do?"

"You'll start at the bottom and learn the business."

"What, like filing or something?"

"That, too, but before you get into the meat of our business, you'll need to understand it from the ground up. You'll work with your grandmother, Juana."

"Juana! But she runs the kitchen and housekeeping."

"Exactly."

"You need *two* people to manage those things?"

"No, just Juana. You'll work for her, doing whatever task she assigns you."

"But she doesn't like me. She'll give me shit jobs."

"All jobs need to be done. And if she doesn't like you, what have you done to make her like you?"

Natalie shrugged. Who cared if Juana liked her or not?

Alejandro smiled. "Don't forget, Nat, dear, that an advantage of us being alike is that I can read your mind."

Natalie rolled her eyes.

"Yeah, roll them, but you know it's the truth. I can get on your wavelength like no one else ever has. Right?"

She said nothing.

"You're thinking that you don't care if Juana likes you or not. Or if anyone else does, either. In a way I agree, but that's not the point. You don't have to care, but you have to know enough to make people useful to you. To do the things you want them to do."

"I'll just order them like you do."

"Ah, that's where you're wrong. I do give orders, and they're obeyed. But people don't just obey because I say something. That kind of obedience is earned."

"So just pay them more."

"Yes, money is a good incentive, but it's not everything."

"Right," her word dripped sarcasm.

"Money isn't the whole answer. You need to build loyalty in other ways as well, or you might find your employee going elsewhere, to someone who offered more money."

"Then just hire someone else."

"But what if they left with more than money? What if they took with them knowledge of your business, something that could hurt if that information fell into the wrong hands?"

"What are you supposed to do? Lie? Gush? Pretend to like them?"

"You can gain loyalty by being polite, being considerate, taking an interest in their lives, being nice."

She wrinkled her nose at that.

"You don't have to like the person. You don't have to feel anything for them. But what you do need to do is understand them, know what makes them tick. Know what it will take to keep them loyal to you. Pretend to like them. Pretend an interest in their lives."

"You're basically telling me to lie."

"If that's what it takes, yes."

Natalie let that digest a minute. "If I work for Juana, she'll give me the worst jobs. She hates me."

"I'm not sure hate is the word I'd use. But it what you call it doesn't matter. If you think she gives you bad jobs because she hates you, make her like you."

"How am I supposed to do *that*?"

"That's what you'll have to figure out."

"Why should I have to do that?" Was that a whine she heard creeping into her voice? She cringed.

"Nat, you have a lot to learn."

She hated it when adults made condescending remarks like that, like they held your youth against you. She turned to leave the room, careful to temper her footsteps. While usually indulgent, one thing Alejandro did not stand was a snit. She'd tried, several times. It always worked with her parents, making them back off. Not with Alejandro, though.

"Oh, and Nat?"

She half-turned at the door.

"Next month you begin college. I've signed you up for the courses I want you to take."

What! She'd just finished the stupid high school courses he insisted she take. She was *done* with school. "But…"

"No buts. This is what you'll do."

"I thought you wanted me to work."

"I do. You'll work for Juana part-time and attend college."

There were ways to draw out online courses. She'd learned all the tricks over the last two years of those dumb high school classes. "Send me the link to the classes and I'll take a look."

"You can see the course outlines online, but you're attending in person."

"What?"

"Yes. You've hidden out from peers long enough. It's time you learned how to rub shoulders with other young people."

The gleam in her eye met his equally determined one.

She backed down first. "What did you sign me up for?"

"Psychology, sociology, philosophy, English and economics."

"I'll hate those!"

Her father shrugged. "Doesn't matter."

"You think that by taking a couple psychology classes I'll understand people?"

"That's the hope, but I might be a bit optimistic. It won't hurt. You need to know what makes people tick if you're going to be able to bend them to your will."

Could this get any worse?

"Just so you know, I have access to all of your courses online and I'll be monitoring your marks. I let you slough off in high school, doing the minimum. That's not good enough for college."

Chapter Thirty-Six

Juana stood in front of her son's desk. He hadn't asked her to take a seat and she didn't presume, just listened carefully. "Do you want me to be easy on her or hard?" It didn't pay with Alejandro to assume; best have it spelled out.

"I want you to be whichever you see fit with her."

They shared a look that made it feel like Alejandro could see into her soul. Did he mean it?

As far as she knew, her son had only a few soft spots. One was for that Natalie brat, one for his brother, and one for the stupid cat that was at this moment windings itself around Juana's ankles. Somehow the thing knew she hated it, so always insisted on rubbing its mangy fur on her. Juana tried not to shudder, knowing how her son felt about showing weakness. Alejandro said the cat's presence was for the benefit of the girls, a calming strategy to keep peace in a household of hormonal women. Juana knew better. If it was the house's pet, why did the thing prefer to spend most of its time beside Alejandro? Or in his lap?

As for Natalie, dare she treat her the way she'd like?

Ever since coming here the girl had been a pain. She might be her own flesh and blood, but that didn't make it less annoying the way she flaunted herself around the place, as if she was better than everyone else. And Alejandro indulged her, spoiling her rotten, letting the girl get away with murder.

"She's my daughter, but I might not always be around to protect her. She needs to start to learn how to take care of herself."

Are you planning on going somewhere?" It didn't do to probe into her son's affairs too deeply. He didn't appreciate it and could shut down questions with just a look. A look was all he needed to imply threat.

"No immediate plans, but it never hurts to be prepared. After all, the world can be a harsh place for a child alone, wouldn't you say, Mother Dearest?"

Juana met his look directly. It didn't pay to be too subservient with Alejandro; that could piss him off just as much as insubordination. She got what he implied.

Yeah, she'd made some choices in her life, maybe the wrong ones, maybe messed up a bit, and paid the price. But she'd done the best she could at the time. If things hadn't worked out the way they did, she'd never have gotten treatment for the breast cancer and wouldn't be here today. As for Alejandro, well, he'd turned out all right. Maybe better than if she'd raised him herself.

But you never know with Natalie. Alejandro was different with that girl. It was almost as if he was blind, saw her as a feminine mini me. He didn't see what she was really like.

He defended her, and the girl traded on that. She acted like her feet didn't stink, that she could do no wrong.

What was Alejandro asking her to do with the girl? Did

he want her brought down a peg or two? If so, Juana was happy to oblige. Or was this a test to see how loyal Juana was? Hard to tell by looking at Alejandro's face. The boy had learned to hide his emotions well. What kind of line to walk here?

"Should I treat her like any new hire?"

"If you think that's best."

He was playing with her; she just knew it. Well, two could play this game. She might be beholden to her son for a roof over her head, a job, and a bigger salary than she'd ever dreamed of earning, but he was still her son. Much of what he was, he'd learned from her. They said that the first four years of life were the most meaningful, didn't they? "Okay. I'll handle Natalie."

Drudgery. Pure drudgery.

Didn't they know who she was? Their boss's daughter, that's who. She was so above them, yet look what that witch, Juana had her doing.

Juana never got her own hands dirty, so why should she?

When Natalie had complained to Alejandro about the chores Juana subjected her to, he said work was good for the soul.

Riiiight. Like sticking your hands in a toilet bowl ever helped anyone's soul. The first time she had to do it, the glove had a hole in it. Natalie just knew that Juana did that on purpose, probably stayed up late the night before, pricking all the gloves she gave Natalie with a pin. Natalie could feel that cerulean blue cleanser eating into her flesh. If it was supposed to melt old urine and whatever stains off the inside of toilets, what would it do to the skin of her hands?

Then the nerve of the woman. She'd inspected and said the job wasn't good enough and made her do it all again.

This was *so* beneath her. Even Howard and Barbara never asked her to do dirty jobs like this. Come to think of it, they hadn't asked her much of anything.

But this Juana had it in for her. She'd hated her from the first day Alejandro brought her home with him. Her granddaughter, her own flesh and blood. What kind of a grandmother would be like that?

It was almost like she was jealous of Natalie's relationship with Alejandro. That thought made Natalie smile. Served her right. Alejandro appreciated smart women. Smart, Juana was not.

Natalie scrubbed away, flinching as some of the cold, blue water seeped in through hole in the gloves. This time she'd double-gloved her hands, but still the foul liquid found its way in. Yeah, for sure Grandma Juana had done this on purpose.

Worse, it wasn't even her own bathroom. It was one of the communal ones used by the girls who stayed here - girls who were stupid enough to get themselves knocked up, then had to rely on the generosity of her father to look after them, find homes for their babies, and make the problem all go away.

How stupid did you have to be to let that happen to you?

A snicker made Natalie look up from swabbing out the last toilet. At the open door stood Marion. Marion the Martyr, Natalie called her. You'd think she was the first woman to ever grow a baby, or at least the first person to feel discomfort when her stomach stuck out two feet more than it was meant to. Marion could go on ad nauseam about all her aches and pains. Natalie had no idea how anyone could stand to be around her. *She* certainly couldn't.

Alejandro had this weird rule. Even though they had a perfectly good private dining room all their own, on Wednesday evenings, he insisted that he and Natalie join the "girls". By girls, he meant the pregnant young women he took in, providing for their medical care, their daily living, and finding adoptive homes for the babies once born. Sort of a full-service adoption agency, with high-end families seeking an infant to bring into their lives.

For the girls, they got a place to live that was better than they'd ever dreamed, and were cared for during their pregnancy, on top of a guarantee that their child would go to a good home. They also got a nice lump sum to help them start their new life post-baby. This residence was such a cushy place, that some girls even showed up a second or third time, as if being a baby-maker was all they could do. For some these losers, that was likely true.

"How the mighty has fallen." Marion the Martyr laughed.

Natalie whipped around. Cutting loose all the pent-up rage at the menial task assigned her by her own grandmother, Natalie heaved the toilet bowl brush at the smirking face in the doorway.

Awkward and slow-moving, or maybe just stupid, Marion didn't even step out of the way. Her smirk changed to shrieks as the bristles caught her in the face. "My eyes, my eyes!" She went wailing down the hallway.

Natalie's turn to smirk.

Chapter Thirty-Seven

It was Wednesday. No excuses. Natalie had tried them all, but nothing short of illness requiring hospitalization was enough to get her out of joining her father at the dinner table of the girls.

The dining room was large, with a table comfortable seating twelve when the residence was at full capacity. Right now, only nine girls stayed with them, seven of them at the table this evening, along with Alejandro at the head of the polished sequoia table, and Natalie at the foot. One girl helped the kitchen staff serve the food; all those in residence took turns rotating through food prep, serving, and house-keeping. Alejandro believed it gave them skills and work experience they could use later in life.

Marion the Martyr arrived a few minutes late, earning a disapproving look from Alejandro. He didn't tolerate tardi-ness; these girls needed to learn discipline.

She came late on purpose; Natalie just knew it. Figures Marion the Martyr would come wearing an eye patch. Must have dug one out of the first aid kit. Just another way to get attention.

After studying Marion for a moment, and the way she glared at Natalie, Alejandro chose to ignore both the eye patch and the late entrance. But his blunt gaze told Marion it had better not happen again.

The food excelled, as usual. Alejandro insisted on it. The clients buying these babies wanted only healthy infants. Although each girl might have begun her pregnancy under dubious circumstances, once they entered this residence, their needs for nutrition, exercise and medical care were well met.

It irked Natalie that they lived so well after they'd screwed up. Alejandro countered that their mistakes were the bread and butter of his business. He also forbade her from using the mocking nicknames she'd come up with for each resident. Couldn't stop her from saying them in her head, though.

It rankled that Alejandro forced her to interact with these girls. Not often, but a meal once a week was annoying as hell. It was also wrong, just plain wrong that Alejandro insisted they eat the same food as was prepared for the girls.

Along the right side of the table came a gagging noise, then Whiny Wanda ran from the table with her hand over her mouth. The sound of retching came from the washroom in the hallway. Whiny Wanda hadn't even had the decency to shut the door before puking.

Catty Cathleen rolled her eyes and picked up her fork.

Annoying Angela glanced toward the hall. "Should I go check on her?"

"No," said Alejandro. "You eat your dinner. Natalie will see to Wanda."

"*Me!* Why should I have to go? Just because she was stupid enough to get herself knocked up and sick, what's that got to do with me?"

Silence. The girls swivelled their heads between Alejandro and Natalie.

Those two locked eyes, Natalie's defiant, Alejandro's determined.

"Natalie, after you apologize to these young women for your rudeness, you will go assist Wanda."

As if. She'd come up against her father's will just a few times before. Normally he indulged her in whatever she wanted, but those rare occasions when he made an edict, she hadn't won. She might be his daughter and heiress, but he held the power.

Clenching the cloth napkin on her lap into tight folds, Natalie lowered her eyes. This wasn't the time or place for a showdown with her father, especially one she was pretty sure she'd lose. "I take it back. I shouldn't have used those words."

As an apology, it was truthful, and as good as it was going to get.

Shoving back her chair, Natalie left with as much dignity as possible. She ignored the little snigger that followed her out of the room. That had to have come from Catty Cathleen. She was always jealous of Natalie's position.

Pausing by the bathroom, she was going to stick her head in, but the stench of vomit pushed itself up her nose. Gross! How could it stink that bad? The girl had only taken a few bites of her meal. "Hey, Wanda. You all right?" There. She'd done her duty.

A gurgled response came back.

"Okay, see you around then." Natalie put as much chirp into her voice as possible. Another idea took form. "Better hurry back or your hamburger will get cold." She was rewarded by more retching sounds. Served Wanda right for getting Natalie in trouble with Alejandro.

Alone in the spacious suite of rooms that they shared, Natalie waited. In the last two years she'd come to know her father well. He'd join her for a little talk, soon.

She'd displeased him. He might frame that as disappointment. Lately, he'd become more critical of her. Sure, they still hung out together and he looked at her with affection, but he'd started to pick at her, as if there were some aspects he didn't like.

Natalie tried to shrug it off. All her life she'd lived with censure. People never understood her, always wanted her to be different. She'd thought that she'd finally ended up with the one person who acknowledged the real Natalie and appreciated her exactly as she was. Lately, though, not so much.

It was almost like he'd decided to take his father role seriously.

She preferred the dad who was fun and didn't care about bettering her, whatever that meant.

The outer door shut, blocking out the rest of the residence from their private sanctum.

Alejandro lowered himself into his recliner of oxblood butter-soft leather. He ran his hand over his face, then studied his daughter.

Natalie aimed for defiant confidence but didn't quite pull it off. This Alejandro was different.

"Nat, you can't do that."

Do what? Her perplexity showed.

"You can't treat people like that."

Like what? "I only said the truth. If they can't face the truth, they'll never make it in life."

"True. That applies to you as well."

What did he mean?

"You see these girls as screw-ups."

Well, duh. Wasn't that obvious?

"Don't judge. If you can't empathize, understand."

"But they *were* stupid. They got themselves knocked up and couldn't take care of themselves."

"Yes, they did. But you don't know what went on in their lives that led them to that point. You were raised in a sheltered environment, by people who cared about you. Not everyone has that luck."

Huh.

"Each of us has wounds that guide our lives, and we don't even realize it."

What? This was a new way of talking for Alejandro.

"Look. We're all shaped by the events in our lives, whether those events are things thrust upon us, or things we had a hand in creating. Doesn't matter how they came about, but they all make us who we are."

"I'm never going to be like *those* girls."

"I pray to God that's true. But you never know what will happen."

"*I'm* sure. I'm not stupid."

"Some of these girls are as bright as you, maybe even brighter. But they've not had your chances."

"They also don't have you for a father." It couldn't hurt to butter him up a little, maybe steer the conversation somewhere less uncomfortable.

"A father." He leaned his head back and closed his eyes.

Almost to himself, he said, "I wonder if I made a mistake bringing you here."

What? No way! These had been the best two years of her life. Was he thinking of sending her back home? No. She was an adult; she didn't have to go.

"Natalie, I might not always be here for you."

"Are you going away?"

"Not if I can help it, but there are no guarantees in life." How to explain this? He didn't want to frighten her, nor did he want to dampen the way she looked up to him. He'd never had anyone look at him that way other than his brother.

"Nat, my business is all about managing people. That means the people who will adopt the babies, as well as the people who will grow the babies. Without either, we'd have no business." He sat forward, lacing his fingers between his knees. "If you're going to be a part of my business, you'll need to know how to manage people. To manage people, you have to understand them."

"I don't like most people."

"I get that. But it doesn't matter if you like them or not, you still have to understand them before you can manage them."

"Okay. I think I get it. That's why you wanted me to take those college courses."

"That's part of the reason." How much to tell her? "You and me, we're different." He pointed his finger between the two of them. "We're loners, not needing a lot of people around us." He needed to convey this gently. "I mean it when I say we're different. This is hard to say, but there's something missing in you and me, something that's hard-wired into other people. See, some people seem to have caring built into them. They like others and feel for them."

Natalie shrugged.

"I know. You don't get it. Can't say that I get this empathy thing either, but it's important. This is the world we live in, and to most of the world caring about others is high on their list of noble traits."

"What do I care what anyone else thinks?"

"You need to care because not caring can get in the way of you getting what you want."

Intriguing.

"Doesn't matter to me if you truly care about others. What does matter to me is that you understand those around you enough so that you can get into their heads. Once you can do that you can bend them to your will."

"Is it necessary?"

"Yes, I'm afraid it is. I'm not sure if I started out this way, or became this way, but like you, I don't care about how others feel. I've had to force myself to learn. This comes instinctively to most people, but for those like you and me, it's something we have to study."

"How did you learn?"

"Trial and error. School of hard knocks. Who knows? I'll admit I'm not good at it, but I do well enough to get by."

"What should I do?"

"Take those classes and internalize what you learn. Start by not being mean."

"I've heard you jump all over someone."

"True. There are times when that's what you need to do. But don't go out of your way to antagonize someone when you have nothing to gain from it." He pulled a cerveza out of the mini fridge disguised as a side table. "Like tonight at supper. You gained nothing by mocking those girls. As I said, don't judge. I can't make you feel empathy for them, but I can expect that you understand where they're coming from. Do you see the difference?"

Natalie nodded. Maybe she saw what he was getting at.

"If you think they're stupid, keep that thought to yourself. If you think they made some dumb moves, think about the shape our business would be in if they hadn't. We'll get more for each of their babies than the average person makes in a year. Understand?" He waited for her response. "We *need* these girls, and others like them."

"I get it."

"How do you think we find these girls, pregnant ones looking for someone else to take their babies?"

Natalie shrugged. Never thought about it.

"Some we find on the streets. More though, come to us by word of mouth. Girls tell other girls how well they're treated here, how they get money to get their lives going after the birth. That's valuable. Do you think they'll keep recommending us if they're mocked while here? Treated badly?"

She hadn't thought about it that way.

Chapter Thirty-Eight

"What's up with you and Juana?"

He'd wondered when this question was coming. Especially now that he'd got Natalie to pay attention to people and dissect her observations. She was getting better at it, although goodness knows how with only him as her teacher. Still, he was all she had, so he'd make the most of it. But this question, this was hitting too close to home.

She waited, her direct gaze telling him she could see him squirming inside. His Natalie didn't shy away from things. Chip off the old block.

"We have a complicated history, Juana and I."

"No kidding. Even *I* can pick up on the tension between you. Let's start easy. Have you always called her Juana?"

"When I was a kid, I called her mom."

"Not mama or madre?"

"We didn't live in Mexico. We were in the US."

"But you're a Mexican citizen."

"Born here, but Juana took us to California, then Minnesota."

"Minnesota? It's cold there."

"Tell me about it," Alejandro mumbled.

Natalie tilted her head. "I sense a story."

"When I was four and my brother two,…"

"Brother? I didn't know you had a brother. How come I've never met this uncle?"

"You will, in time. Now do you want this story or not?" If she wanted to go off topic, that was fine with him. This could wait for another time, or never.

"I want it."

"Anyway, Janice…"

"Janice?"

"When we were in America, she wanted us to use American-sounding names. She was Janice, Matteo was Matt, and I was called Alex."

"Ah, like she calls me Natalia."

"Right. Anyway, Janice had a boyfriend who moved to Minnesota and asked her to come join him. So, she packed us up and drove there."

"He must have liked kids to take on two little boys."

"He didn't know about us."

"Oh, joy."

"Pretty much, and it went downhill from there. Luke hadn't bargained on kids hampering his style. He had a job, but it was seasonal, with no money coming in that winter. So, Janice had to work in a diner. Nothing pleasant about those times for any of us. Long story short, Matt and I were in the way, and they wanted to be rid of us. I think Janice resisted, but then she found a lump in her breast, thought she had cancer and was going to die."

"Cancer doesn't mean certain death these days."

"When you have no insurance or money for treatment it can. Anyway, she thought she was dying and there was no one to look after Matt and me. She heard scary things about foster care, and so thought we'd be better off dead than in the system."

"And you say *I* need to get better at making choices."

"Exactly. Maybe it's a flaw in our genetics."

"What happened?"

"Mommy Dearest and old Luke took us to some isolated road, stashed us in a snowbank and drove away."

"Holy cow! What's Juana say about this now?"

"She says she did what she thought was best for us at the time, thought it would be a painless way to go, and better than risking what might happen to us in foster care."

"Riiight."

"Yeah, I know."

"Someone obviously found you."

"No. I hadn't taken the juice Mom made for us. She used to give us stuff to knock us out; cheaper than getting a babysitter.

"I waited for them to come back for us, but when they didn't, I dragged Matt down the road until I found a farmhouse."

"Pretty impressive for a four-year-old."

"Not really. As I dragged him, I lost one of Matt's boots and socks. When we got to the house, I couldn't make enough noise to get anyone to come to the door. So, we slept on their porch. They found us in the morning, but by then Matt's foot was badly frozen and one of my hands." He held up the hand that was missing two fingers.

"And Matt?"

"He lost most of one foot."

"What about Juana?"

"Eventually our identity was discovered, and Juana and

Luke were arrested. They both got five years for child neglect and endangerment."

"Five years for almost killing two kids?"

Alejandro shrugged. "That's the value the courts put on our lives."

"Were you in foster care?"

"Not for long. For a bit a couple who'd befriended Juana and us took us in. But then the woman got hurt in a fall and couldn't look after us anymore. We eventually got sent back here to Elena, our grandmother."

"Was that good?"

"What's good? We survived."

"Let me get this straight. When you were just a kid your mother tried to kill you. Now you take her in and give her a job."

"She's family."

"If that's how family treats you, you don't need enemies." She waited a moment. "But you've done all right for yourself."

"There's a German philosopher named Friedrich Nietzsche. He said, "One must still have chaos in oneself to be able to give birth to a dancing star.""

He let that sink in. "I said before that we're different, you and me. Maybe Juana, too. We don't feel the same things as other people, or at least it doesn't come naturally to us. Some might say that we have more chaos inside us, less feeling, less connection to others. But that doesn't mean we're damaged or wrong. Just different. We can still succeed, but we might have to work at it harder."

"Still…"

"I learned to make my own way, make my own worth. We all deserve respect. If the world doesn't respect us in the way we'd like, we should at least respect ourselves. I did what I had to do to earn that respect."

Natalie retired to her room, leaving Alejandro alone with his thoughts, thoughts he'd done his best to bury deep. If it wasn't for Natalie's need to understand, he'd never let them see the light of day.

Alejandro spent his life trying to erase the image of the unworthy child he was, left along the side of the road like unwanted trash. No, he didn't die that night in the frigid Minnesota winter. Neither did his disabled brother whom he dragged to shelter.

Now Alejandro made his own worth, his own rules.

Chapter Thirty-Nine

Alejandro read the encrypted message sent by his IT security guy. Not good. Their firewall had been breached yet again. He hired the best, but someone was better. The only ones with the resources to do this had to be governments, both here and north of the border.

It was his own fault. He'd crossed the line when he tried to take the child of Natalie's neighbor in San Diego. It was one thing when parents voluntarily handed over their kids, as Sally had done, but snatching someone else's kid was wrong. He'd known it at the time, and it was reinforced all the more now that he had a daughter of his own in his care, but he got greedy. The money offered was too good to pass up. He'd escaped, yeah, but just barely. Officials had been sniffing around his operation even before then, but that blunder put him squarely in their radar.

The other problem was Anna. His ex-wife. She'd led the officials right to his mansion when she tried to rescue Sally's daughter, Bonnie. She'd succeeded, too, bringing the cops down on his head. He'd barely escaped, and it had taken years to build his business back to even a fraction of what it had been.

Now, they were after him again.

He had more to lose this time, more than just his money and freedom. He had Natalie, his responsibility.

He could feel the noose tightening. The end was inevitable. But Natalie wasn't ready to be on her own. She had so much yet to learn, was so vulnerable. How much time did he have? Didn't matter. He'd do what had to be done.

Alejandro'd told Juana to rotate Natalia through all the jobs. That meant she couldn't keep the girl on toilet duty forever. Alejandro would check. One thing he knew was, that was thorough.

Yes, her son was diligent.

He was successful. That had to mean she'd done something right. Right?

Yeah, she hadn't been the perfect mother, but who was?

Life had been hard back then, truly hard. Try as she might, stuff just didn't work out for her. Somehow, the gods conspired against her.

She'd risked it all, leaving her home in Rosarito and moving to California. That took guts. Once settled, and after a little play time, which she deserved, she'd gone back for the boys and brought them to live with her. Not easy to be a single mother in San Diego, without any family around to help.

But she'd done it. And even made some good friends in Olivia and Jerry. They'd been a real help with the boys, given the kids a taste of what true grandparents could be like.

She stilled in her dusting. *She* was a grandmother now that Alejandro had brought Natalie to live with them. And how was that going?

Objectively, she was a better abuela than Elena had been. But she was no Olivia, nor a Phoebe. That was all right. They couldn't expect her to be. Those other women had it easy; life smiled on them, plus they had good men to support them. Juana had tried to find good men - even one would have done, but just like Elena, she was cursed to hook up with bad ones, ones who expected *her* to support *them*. It was supposed to be the other way around. Things like that took a toll on a person, changed you.

Some people sailed through life easily, everything falling into their laps. Others had to work for it, for every little tidbit of luck.

When things were hard, you had to make tough choices. That had been Juana's plight. Every turn she made, the choices were hard.

But she'd stepped up. She'd taken responsibility for herself and her boys. She'd worked at menial jobs to support them. When she'd faced imminent death from cancer, she'd weighed the options for her sons. Lives of suffering, or quick, painless deaths. Maybe not everyone would understand - the courts certainly hadn't but falling gently to sleep and never waking up was kinder than how their lives might have turned out in the system.

Many would judge her, but she stood by her decision as being the best she could do at the time.

Besides, if life hadn't turned out the way it did, she'd never have received the medical treatment that spared her life.

And Alejandro. He'd turned out well, a son to be proud of. Maybe a touch of adversity had strengthened him. He was richer than Midas and ran an empire. Granted, that empire was on a reduced scale since that Anna person had brought the authorities on them. But Alejandro had risen from the ashes, rebuilding, and bringing Juana with him.

That had to mean she hadn't been a bad mother, didn't it?

Now he was bringing his daughter into this. Maybe that was okay, but the girl was hard to warm up to. A snooty little thing.

She didn't look so high and mighty up to her elbows in toilets. It hadn't taught the child humility though; if anything, she looked at Juana with even more disdain.

But Juana had to switch Natalia to something else, or risk Alejandro's wrath. *Everyone* wanted to avoid that, especially Juana. She was well aware of the lifestyle she enjoyed now, and how that could instantly disappear if she displeased her son. She feared that testing the limits of his maternal devotion would not work in her favor. Not worth risking losing the sanctum she had here.

So, she complied.

But she could do little things. Her mother taught her that you needed to fit in wherever you were. Born Juana, she switched to the English version of her name, Janice, when living north of the border. Her sons got used to their anglicized names when in California and Minnesota. Why shouldn't Natalie do the same?

Natalie hated when Juana called her Natalia and tried to ignore her. Blatant rudeness was something Alejandro didn't tolerate, and he made Natalie answer to her Mexican variant of her name. Somehow, Juana found many occasions to emphasize the additional syllable, Natalia.

Natalia served time in the kitchen. For several days she peeled potatoes. Then she chopped tomatoes endlessly.

But behind Juana's back, the chef took pity on Natalia. Camila ruled the kitchen with benevolence. As long as you met her exacting standards, she remained sunny and encouraging. If she caught wind you were taking shortcuts with either the food ordering or preparation, look out. Juana learned the hard way.

Somehow, Camila saw Natalie's surliness as insecurity. She taught the girl proper knife techniques, and rapidly moved her on to more and more involvement in the prep work, and then the cooking. Who would have thought the kid would take to kitchen work?

When Natalia began cooking private meals for herself and her father, Juana caught on to her game. Just another way to worm her way into Alejandro's good graces. This was confirmed when Alejandro informed Juana that Camila would now take over assigning Natalie's duties.

Chapter Forty

Carefully lining his knife and fork across his now empty plate, Alejandro pushed back from the table. "Delicious. Absolutely delicious."

Natalie did a poor job of pretending not to care about his praise.

Watching her, Alejandro realized his daughter needed more practice in accepting compliments. She acted like they didn't matter, but they did. He'd work on that. Just one more thing added to the list. Parenting was tougher than it looked, especially when many lessons needed to be crammed into a short span of time.

"You and Camila have become close."

Natalie shrugged. "I spend a lot of time in her kitchen."

"It shows." He nodded at his plate. "You've picked up a lot in a short time."

"It's not hard."

"I started off with Juana in charge of the kitchen, but soon learned we needed someone else."

"Not surprising, with that c…"

Alejandro held up his hand. "Respect. Remember that."

"Why should I? What is there to respect about her?"

"She's your grandmother."

"Huh. That's just a word. She's never done anything grandmotherly toward me and she certainly wasn't a good mother to you."

"She is what she is. She's still your grandmother, so you will speak to her with respect." That was non-negotiable.

Natalie leaned forward in her chair. "I don't get it. How can you be nice to her? She tried to kill you!"

"'After facing the past and finding self-forgiveness, it becomes easier to forgive others.' Ever heard that saying?"

"Is that what you did with Juana?" Natalie asks.

He nodded. "She did the best she could at the time."

"But…"

"I know. It's not the solution you might have found, or me, or many people. She went with the options she saw."

"It was wrong!"

"Natalie, have you ever done something wrong?"

She studied her plate. "Maybe. Depends on your definition of wrong."

He let that go. For now. "My dear, you need a code."

She wrinkled her brow.

"Something you can live by. A code with lines you won't cross. To some people, that line is obvious, ingrained in them, something they don't have to think about." He steepled his hands under his chin. How to explain this? "For people like you and me, and maybe Juana, we don't have an automatic sense of that line. It's too easy to get caught up in what we want, what we're after. We need to think about it and create a code to live by."

"How?"

"You're taking a step toward it with your college classes.

Study people. Study society and the rules that make it work."

"I don't care about their stupid rules."

"You must. Like it or not, you are part of society, even if you consider yourself a loner. Think of it as self-preservation. Communities develop rules to keep them functioning. Cross those rules, and you'll find yourself in trouble."

Natalie scoffed. "I've been in trouble all my life."

"Kid stuff. And you had parents to protect you from the worst of it. You're no longer a kid so the consequences of breaking society's rules can be severe."

"Not if you have enough money to cushion things."

"Even then. No one is above the law."

"*Suuure*. People get away with stuff all the time, especially rich people."

"For a while. But when they fall, they fall hard." Just so she knew, he added, "And you're not that rich."

"Do you follow the rules?"

"I do now." Now that he had a daughter to care for. "I haven't always. That code I talked about? Sometimes I forgot that, got carried away, tempted by money and power."

"You're still here. Nothing bad happened."

Not yet. "Some of my actions caused problems for me. I lost an estate and much of my business when I got too greedy and too cocky."

"But you're fine now."

"I've rebuilt things, but the business is not as lucrative as it once was."

"Is it legit?"

"It is now. We run a legitimate adoption agency and residence for girls with unwanted pregnancies."

"Would you make more money if you were only semi-legit."

His gaze was level. "Yes."

Natalie pondered this. "So, it's that code thing?"

He nodded.

"I'm willing to take the risk if we can make more money other ways."

"Nope. We're not going there."

"But…"

"No! I've tried that. Apart from the legal ramifications, it does something to your soul."

A laugh escaped Natalie's lips. "I had a teacher once who said I didn't have a soul."

Alejandro studied his daughter. Howard and Barbara had not been on the ball when raising this young girl. They needed to do better.

He'd always dreaded people seeing him as he really was - a frightened, unwanted little boy, tossed aside as worthless. That led him to do things he was not necessarily proud of, things that gave him value in his own eyes. To him, value had equated with money. Now that Natalie was in his care, his goals changed.

It was a lot to take in; these lessons had taken him years to learn, and now unlearn. He could hardly expect Natalie to get it right away. But his time with her might be short.

"You need friends."

"Huh. I've got along perfectly fine without friends."

"That's because you had Barbara and Howard, and now me, to shelter you. But someday you'll be on your own."

"I don't need friends."

"No one functions totally alone. Even a hermit in the woods interacts with people when he goes in for supplies.

You, my dear, don't strike me as the type to rough it in a cabin in the woods."

She smirked.

"What if I'm not around?"

"You're not even 40 yet."

"Doesn't matter. Things happen." Judging by the attempts to penetrate his firewall, the sanctum he'd created was threatened. "You need people to work for you, to work *with* you, people you can trust."

"Pay them enough and they'll do anything."

"If you rely on money alone, they could go to the highest bidder." He could see she wasn't convinced. "You've made friends with Camila."

"I don't know about friends, but we hang together in the kitchen."

"That's what friends do - spend time bonding over a shared interest."

Was that embarrassment on her face? "I like learning about cooking, and Camila's fun."

"That's a friend. Friends add an extra dimension to your life. Someone who genuinely likes you. Someone you can trust." This next part he knew she wouldn't like. "We're getting a new resident tomorrow. Her name's Evaline. She's been here before."

Natalie rolled her eyes. "Another one of those losers who can't figure out where babies come from."

Alejandro leaned forward on his elbows. "The first time she was at one of my residences, she was two years younger than you, pregnant from her long-time boyfriend. Her parents threw her out for disgracing them. The boyfriend ran off. She was on the streets with no place to stay, no way to support herself."

"Well, what did she expect?"

Speaking over top of her, Alejandro continued. "This time, she's in college. *Your* college, to be exact, taking second year classes, working nights to pay her way since there's no one to help support her. She was on her way home from work late one evening when she was attacked. Beaten and raped." He let that sink in. "After getting out of the hospital, she found she'd lost her job. On top of that, she was pregnant."

Natalie said nothing.

"Evaline's arranged to continue some of her classes online. She'll do that here."

"Okay. What's that got to do with me."

"You will befriend her."

"Me? Why?" And how?

"She's alone and frightened and still recovering from her injuries. You have something in common, your studies. She's a bright girl, one who stands out from the hundreds of others who've come through my residences." He stood up from the table. "You need practice at making friends. She'll arrive tomorrow in the late afternoon; you'll greet her, help her get settled with her things, show her around, and stay with her until bedtime."

Chapter Forty-One

It wasn't so bad. The worst was figuring out what to say. But Evaline helped and didn't make Natalie carry the whole conversational burden. Evaline had lots of questions, plus she explained how this residence differed from the last one she'd been in. She talked about when the police raided the former place, how she and Juana had escaped through a hidden staircase, only to fall into the hands of the officials.

"They saw me and the other girls as victims, so treated us well. They gave us a place to stay and some money, offered us work training."

"Why did they raid the place?" This was news to Natalie.

"Didn't you know? Alejandro ran an illegal baby market." As Natalie's eyes widened, she hurried to explain. "Oh, he treated us well. He had to. The people buying our babies wanted only healthy infants, so he fed and housed us in style, better than any of us had ever experienced. We all saw the doctor regularly. After the baby was born, we got to stay for two weeks to recover, then he sent us on our way with bus fare, the address of the apartment he'd found for us in the city of our choice, and enough cash to live on for three months."

"Illegal? I thought it was within the law to run an adoption agency."

"It is, and especially now, he does everything above board. I never heard the reason, but something changed about two years ago, and he stopped with the questionable stuff. It's still all hush hush, though."

"Why's that?"

"Alejandro escaped in that raid. The officials on both sides of the border are still after him."

Interesting. Worrisome, too. How did that fit in with the code Alejandro talked about, or was the code something new?

Camila allowed Evaline into the kitchen after learning that the young woman had worked in a restaurant doing far more than waiting tables. It was nice. The three of them settled into easy camaraderie, preparing the evening meals under Camila's direction. Rather than a chore, Natalie found it a relaxing way to end her day of studying.

And study she did.

She'd always been an indifferent student. School was a place to tolerate. Maybe it wouldn't have been so bad if there were no other students. She didn't get the kids, never had, right from kindergarten. Their games, the way they liked to hang out together, the things they thought funny were all a mystery. When they realized that she didn't understand, that she didn't fit in, they shunned her.

Who cared? She didn't need them and their stupid

games with stupid rules anywhere. She was happier on her own.

She was happy each time some school kicked her out - the longer the suspension, the better. Finally, an expulsion ended the daily school grind. Her parents, taking pity on her for what they saw as unfair treatment, allowed her to stay home. She needed a break from all the stress.

When they moved to a new area to give her "a fresh start", it wasn't hard to pretend to be too traumatized to consider starting over at a new school. She played that card as long as she could, until finally, her parents hired a neighbor to tutor her.

That was mildly amusing since there was another girl receiving tutoring at the same time, a silent girl who was easy to torment because she couldn't tell anyone. It became a game to see how far she could go.

There were younger kids around, too, ones who at first looked up to Natalie as a teenager, a babysitter. Even though she didn't *like* kids, the flattery was nice, something she'd never experienced before.

But the silent girl, Bonnie, hung around too. Bonnie knew the little kids and they doted on her. Sneaky Bonnie quietly wooed the children away from Natalie, until they told their parents they didn't want Natalie babysitting them. Especially that mouthy kid, Amy, making up stories about Natalie.

That kid babbled on incessantly, even when she wasn't tattling on Natalie. They got their own back, though, she and Alejandro. When one of his adoptive clients put in a request for a seven-year-old girl, they'd snatched Amy.

In the end, it hadn't worked out and she and Alejandro fled the country. It was exciting, really. She'd played a major role in their escape, proving herself to her biological father.

Ever since then they'd been together. Her read dad, a man who understood her.

But Alejandro told her what they'd done had been wrong. They could have gotten in a lot of trouble for it, him doing jail time, and her most likely in juvenile detention. Now, *that* sounded unpleasant.

Alejandro said that apart from the risk to their own hides, taking the kid, even an annoying kid, from her mother had been morally wrong. That was different than finding homes for unwanted babies. He'd crossed over the line with that scheme and wouldn't do so again.

Didn't seem so bad to Natalie, but he'd jumped all over her when she said so. She knew when to keep her mouth shut.

And when not to. Several times a week, Alejandro quizzed her about her university classes, discussing the points she learned in psychology, sociology and philosophy. He was less interested in her economics and accounting classes, simply saying he expected her to do well in those. But he insisted that all five would be needed if she was to help him run his business.

After finding out that Evaline had also studied sociology and psychology, he often included her in their discussions. At first Natalie resented the intrusion into their private time. But it was okay. Evaline was fun to hang with and she had a different take on some of the topics than Natalie had gleaned. Discussing how people thought and why they did things was sort of interesting. Strange, but interesting.

As was having a friend.

Chapter Forty-Two

Leaning against the doorway to the main kitchen, Alejandro observed his daughter. This Natalie seemed lighter, happier. Sure, she'd laughed with him, and they'd had some good times together in the past, but this was different. This was Nat with a peer.

Evaline was good for her. Close in age, but wiser in life experiences. Wiser in the way of people, as well. She shared her views with Natalie, not looking down on her when Nat clearly required explanations for things that would have come naturally to Evaline.

Camila, too, was patient with Nat. Explaining, guiding, and complimenting the young girl on her growing skills. Their conversation wasn't just relegated to cooking, either. He'd eavesdropped shamelessly; how else was he to keep up with how his daughter progressed?

The young women's laughter filled the room, and Evaline and Natalie bumped hips together.

Alejandro backed out of the room before they even knew he was there.

After supper, Natalie and Evaline joined him in his private parlour. They were discussing the concept of family, as explained in Nat's sociology textbook.

"It says, '...the comfort of your identity can only be found in the environment in which it was created.'" Natalie read aloud. "What's that supposed to mean?"

As Evaline explained her thoughts on that statement, Alejandro's mind wandered. How did that apply to his daughter? Sure, he was happy to have her around, and she seemed to enjoy being with him. But was she losing out by not being around the people who'd raised her for the first sixteen years of her life? The foundation of her existence was with them.

Could she create a new identity here with him? Would that negate those important growing up years?

Life with him might be tenuous, how it ended out of his control. He never used to worry much about the law; he could easily lose himself again as he'd done many times before.

But that was when he was alone. No responsibilities other than himself, and financially to his brother. It was different having a daughter. He didn't want a life on the lam for her, nor did he want to risk the possibility of imprisonment for her.

Family was the wellspring of the best of us and the worst of us.

Look at Evaline. Even though her family tossed her out when she really needed their help, she still missed them, still spoke of them fondly, and hoped to one day be reunited with them.

She'd forgiven them. Sort of like he'd forgiven Juana,

although he suspected the similarities were slight. Evaline seemed to genuinely understand why her family abandoned her, and no longer held it against them. She could see things from their perspective, even though she said that she'd never do such a thing to a kid of her own.

Well, Alejandro would never leave a child of his own in a snowbank to freeze to death. Still, he understood why Juana had done what she'd done, at least partly understood. Most of us do the best we can at the time with the tools available to us. Didn't make certain choices right, but it was what it was.

Yes, family was the wellspring of the best of us and the worst of us.

Because of his early experiences, Alejandro fought to be worth something. Did he always fight in the best way? No, but he was trying to be a better person for his daughter's sake.

It got harder and harder to maintain his callous exterior. Maybe age played a role, and he no longer needed to put up the indifferent front now that he was successful.

He felt things for other people now, genuine feelings.

He owed something to his abuela, Elena, for taking in him and his brother as kids. He still regretted running away from her when he was sixteen. But the pressure had become too much, trying to be the man of the house, trying to go to school, and work, and look after Matteo. Elena certainly didn't.

Through the lens of someone doing the best they could at the time, Elena might not have done such a bad job. She'd taken them in when no one else would. She'd shared her home with them, such as it was, and whenever she had food, she shared that as well. But at sixteen, he couldn't take it anymore and fled.

By the time he was eighteen, he regularly sent money to Elena, hoping the cash went to buy food for her and Matteo, rather than lining the pockets of the owner of Elena's favorite watering hole, only to finally find out that Matteo was no longer with her.

Once he became an adult, he'd researched his family - Elena, Juana, and Matteo. Elena was just where he'd left her but wizened beyond her years. He hired a local woman to bring his abuela meals once a day and try to keep an eye on her. It must have worked, because he stopped hearing rumors of his grandmother sleeping in the street.

It took several months to locate Matteo's whereabouts. He'd been sent to an institution. There were good institutions and poor institutions. Money was often the deciding factor. Now that Alejandro had money, Matteo resided in the best place his older brother could find, paid for with iron-clad annuities that would fund Matteo for the rest of his life. Not that Matt understood any of that, but Alejandro did. Family mattered. Look after your brother.

Researching Juana took more work. She was famous when she first went to prison, the story of how she left her two little boys to die in a snowstorm making the news on both sides of the border. After she'd served her time, the news followed her, or tried to, but she disappeared. It was almost twenty years later that Alejandro finally tracked her down. At first his hunt for his mother was fuelled by thoughts of revenge. Over time, his hatred of her settled down into dislike with a tinge of understanding.

Her life had not been easy, either before that fateful night, or afterward. No one wanted to hire an ex-con, especially one who'd tried to murder her children. Slipping back over the border into Mexico and reverting to the name Juana helped.

For a while after he uncovered her whereabouts, Alejandro was content with updates on her life. But she struggled. Were her struggles partly because of him? What if he'd been a better child? What if he'd helped more with Matt? If he hadn't been such a burden, would she have still tried to off him? Even when he had no parental feelings himself, he knew intellectually that killing your kid was rarely the first solution that came to a parent's mind. Now that he had a daughter of his own, he understood that most parents would give their life for their kid.

So, through a broker, he contacted his mother, making her an offer of a job. Heaven knew what she could bring to his organization, but there must be something.

She was family, and he owed her. He didn't have to love her, didn't even have to like her, but he could look after her. She'd joined the staff on his previous estate, helping to look after the stable of girls staying there. She wasn't kind to the girls, but she wasn't cruel, either. She was there, and she did her job. What more could you ask of the woman?

Those first few months were awkward, with Juana on the defensive, as if just waiting for Alejandro to spew his hatred of her, his resentment of what she'd done to him. But he didn't. Initially, it was a game, keeping her on edge, waiting for the other shoe to drop. Gradually, he saw her as an old woman, one who'd made mistakes and mostly had a pitiful life. He'd look after her, as a son should.

When the police raided the estate, Juana'd been caught. She pled ignorance of the true nature of what went on in the walled compound, saying she just did some cleaning and cooking. They didn't believe her. She did a little time, not much.

She had enough money banked that she was fine, as long as she lived frugally.

By the time Alejandro got his business back up and running again, her bank balance crept down to concerning levels. But Alejandro sent for her, and she'd lived and worked at this estate ever since.

Juana didn't know it, but Alejandro had a pension set aside for his mother. If anything happened to him, lawyers would contact Juana, giving her access to the account that would support her the rest of her life.

But Juana would not be able to touch the money set aside for Matteo. Never. There were limits to how far Alejandro trusted their mother.

Chapter Forty-Three

It was Saturday morning. Alejandro rapped on Natalie's door. "Get up, Nat. We're going someplace. Meet me at me car in half an hour."

No discussion. No "do you want to..." from her father. Natalie knew that tone of voice. This was not optional.

Half an hour later, bolstered by her shower and two cups of the best coffee Mexico grew, Natalie was in the passenger seat of Alejandro's Mastretta MXT sports car, the one outward trapping of luxury he allowed himself. So far, Nat had not been allowed to drive it. Her jeep was fine, and did the job, but without the swank of the Mastretta.

"Where are we going?"

"Villa de Juarez."

Okay. "Why? What's there?"

"Your uncle."

Well, that was a surprise. "How long will it take us to get there?"

"About an hour."

He wasn't being very forthcoming. "What's my uncle do there?"

"Do? I guess you could say he's retired. Relaxes and enjoys himself." To distract her, Alejandro signalled, then pulled over to the side of the road. "Want to drive?"

"Do I!"

Natalie drove carefully, doing nothing to cause Alejandro to take back his offer. But it wasn't easy, with the gas pedal so sensitive.

Reaching over, Alejandro turned on the cruise control, setting it at exactly the speed limit. Might be less fun for Natalie, but he couldn't risk them getting stopped for a traffic violation.

Following his directions, Natalie turned off the highway, up a long, windy, inclined driveway, landscaped with compact pine and oak trees. She stopped as stately, shiny black wrought iron gates blocked the road, with similar fencing extending as far as she could see both to the left and the right. In the middle of the road, about ten feet before the gate was a concrete pillar, about four feet high.

"Drive up to the pillar, then hold this up to the screen." He handed her a plastic card.

The card reader gave a beep, then the gates retracted to the sides. Natalie drove on through. After about another twenty feet, the trees gave way to manicured lawns and gardens, trellises with trailing bougainvillea in shades of white, pink and red. Everywhere the vegetation outdid that of a botanical garden. "What is this place?"

"It's where your Uncle Matteo lives, along with some of his friends."

A sprawling building appeared, a three-storey central structure, with wings on either side going out, then back. Looking around, Natalie could see where to leave the car.

"Pull up to the front door, under the portico. Someone will be out to take care of the car."

Within seconds of turning off the ignition, a uniformed valet appeared by Natalie's window. He opened the door for her, holding out his hand for the keys, his other gloved hand, gently taking Natalie's arm to help her from the car. Looking over the roof to Alejandro, he said, "Good to see you again, sir. I hope you enjoy your visit."

"I'm certain we will. This is my daughter, Natalie. You'll be seeing her often."

Natalie shot a look at her father.

"Very good sir. Welcome to both of you." He got in the Mastretta and drove carefully around the building and out of sight.

"You trust a stranger with your car?" This was the first time he'd allowed *her* to drive it.

"He's not a stranger."

Taking her arm, Alejandro led her to the massive double entry door where a butler stood in honest to good-ness tie and tails. She'd only seen such attire in movies.

"Good day, sir. Lovely to have you with us. Mr. Matteo will be delighted to see you. I believe he's in the greenhouse."

Alejandro led Natalie down a series of wide marble halls, everything gleaming. They passed a formal dining room and some sitting areas with people in wheelchairs. Behind closed sliding doors they heard a woman singing, accompanied by a piano, while someone else thumped away on the same instrument, much the way a toddler might.

They passed people in the hall who nodded and smiled but kept on their way. At one point, an older woman came right up to them, stopping in front of Alejandro and putting her hands around his face. He just stood there, tolerating it. Natalie prayed she wouldn't try to touch her. What was this place?

Alejandro tenderly removed the woman's hands and guided the lady to a sofa in a nearby room. He lifted her feet onto an ottoman and patted her knee. Then they returned to their journey down the hallway.

Their steps ended at a glassed-in enclosure The marble floor gave way to terracotta once they pushed the bar to gain entry into the greenhouse. Tinted glass panes lined the three soaring walls, meeting at the glass panels that made up the ceiling. Fans controlled the humidity and temperature. A sanctum for those loving the scent of lush plantings.

A central bunker, plus the two outer walls held three-foot high flower beds. The scent of greenery and growing things filled the moist air. At the far end of the room a bunker held only soil and gardening tools. Seated in a wheelchair in front of it was a man. He used a trowel to fill a small pail, emptied it, then started over again.

"Gardening again, I see," said Alejandro.

The man turned. It took a few seconds for recognition to dawn, then he dropped his tools, his face breaking into a mega grin. Using only his feet, the man propelled himself forward, bouncing in his chair with each pull. "A.., A...," he said. At least that's what Natalie interpreted from the sounds coming from the guy's mouth.

Letting go of her arm, Alejandro hurried forward, bending, and wrapping his arms around the man.

The guy wound his arms around Alejandro's neck and didn't let go.

Finally, laughing, Alejandro disengaged the man's arms, placing the guy's hands in his lap. Reaching into his pocket,

Alejandro withdrew a handkerchief and gently rubbed the spittle from the man's cheek. "Matteo," he said, "I'd like you to meet your niece, Natalie." He gestured for Nat to come forward.

Was he kidding? What if this guy grabbed her?

Alejandro's eyes commanded her to obey.

Slowly she took steps toward the brothers, stopping partly behind her father.

"Do you want to give him a hug or a handshake?"

What? Was he out of his mind? Searching his face, she saw that he wasn't. But the guy was huge, much bigger than Alejandro. Would he hurt her? And he drooled. How could she touch someone like that?

Alejandro's arm propelled her toward her uncle.

Obliging, Natalie held her breath and leaned into the man, putting her left arm around his shoulders. This close, she breathed in the faint scents of aftershave and shampoo. At least he didn't stink. She felt the guy's big hand pat her back. She counted to three, then pulled away. Watching Alejandro, she felt like she'd passed a test. Barely.

A soft knock, then the greenhouse door opened. A uniformed worker entered, carrying two padded chairs. "Would you like these, sir?"

"Thank you," replied Alejandro.

The man positioned the chairs on either side of Matteo, facing the loamy soil. From a cupboard he pulled two more pails and trowels. "For you and the miss, sir." He stood back. "If you want anything else, Mr. Matteo has his pager clipped to his shirt."

Alejandro put his flat hand in front of his mouth, then tilted his hand down. He nudged Matteo do to the same. The staffer reciprocated the movement, then left.

Matteo was already busy filling and emptying his pail.

Alejandro seated himself and joined in the task, signaling Natalie to do the same. For the next half hour there was no conversation, just sounds from Matteo.

There was something soothing about the repetitive, meaningless task.

Chapter Forty-Four

Back on the road, this time with Alejandro driving, Natalie broke the silence. "What was that thing you did with your hand, all three of you?"

"That's how you say thanks in sign language."

Natalie digested this. "Doesn't he talk?"

"No. He has other ways to communicate."

"What's wrong with him?"

"Do you mean what's different about him?" Alejandro's glance defied any argument about the choice of words.

Natalie nodded.

"He has Sotos Syndrome. You've probably never heard of it. It causes the child to grow quickly; when he was two, he was bigger than me and I was two years older than him. Sotos also causes delays in mental and physical abilities. As you saw, his mind hasn't progressed past that of a child."

"Can he walk?"

A sore point. "He didn't as a toddler, but who knows if he might have eventually? He lost most of one foot after that night we spent in the snowstorm. That was on me. If

I'd only noticed that we'd lost his boot, then his sock, things might have been different for him. Maybe he'd be walking today."

"I don't think that was *your* fault. You were a little kid yourself."

"I was older. You're supposed to take care of your little brother and I failed."

"So, you're making up for it now."

Then went another twenty miles down the road before either spoke again.

"Responsibility for Matteo's care will fall to you if anything happens to me," Alejandro said.

"Me?"

"You're his family. That's why you needed to meet him today. There's an account set up with sufficient funds to provide for Matteo as long as he lives. You might need to administer the account, but the money's all there, enough for any eventualities."

"Why me? He has a mother."

Alejandro just looked at her. "Would you leave his finances and care in Juana's hands?"

"I get your point." Natalie sat in silence a few minutes. "But you're young. You'll be around a long time, probably outlive your brother. Why are you telling me about this?"

"It pays to be prepared. You never know what the future holds, so I've secured Matteo's care. If I'm not around, you'll need to visit him at least once a month, and keep in touch with the staff about how he's doing. Understand?"

Natalie nodded. There'd be ways around this.

They stopped for a coffee along the way home. Sitting in a booth in the corner, with no one around was a good time to have that talk. At home he was never sure when Juana might be listening in.

"Let's talk money."

"Okay." Natalie never gave it much thought, other than recognizing it was obvious Alejandro had lots of the stuff.

"When I'm gone, you'll inherit everything. Some things are set up, like Matteo's care, a lifetime annuity for Juana, money to help Evaline through university. I've set aside money to pay off Howard and Barbara's house."

"Why would you do that? They both have jobs."

"To thank them for raising my daughter and taking good care of her. They're your family."

"Adoptive family. You're my real family."

"Family is family, whether through genetics or choice. There's also an educational fund set up for your little brother."

Her dad had thought of everything.

"You'll have a choice. There's enough money to support you if you decide to never work a day in your life. I'd be disappointed if that was the route you took, but it's up to you.

"You can be as hands-on in our business as you want. If you prefer to have nothing to do with it, managers will handle things for you. I'll warn you though, that trusting it to strangers could have things get away on you. But that'll be up to you. Your career choice is just that. No strings."

"I won't want to sit around on my duff all day. I like the idea of business, so I'll probably work with you."

"If I'm not around, you'll have choices, but I'd prefer that you do something. Be bold. Go for your dreams. It's easier when you have enough money to cushion your fall if something doesn't work out, and not all things you'll attempt will work."

"I'm smart. I'll *make* things work."

Alejandro fiddled with his spoon. "Good to be confident, but life does things. You know, there's a smart guy named Stephen Dunne. Something he said resonated with me years ago:

We are human. We have doubts. We have fears that if we try to live out our dreams and fail, we will have to live the rest of our lives without a dream and with self-loathing. What a risk we say...So we try to lessen or eliminate the risk. A common approach to lessening the risk is to wait for the right moment. And that moment never comes. Because the paradox is that that moment has to be made by taking the risk.

"That's the quote you have on the wall by your desk."
He nodded.
"I'm not sure I get it."
"When we get home, read it. Read it every day, until it sinks in."

Raising his coffee cup to his lips, Alejandro regarded his daughter. "Have you enjoyed your life here these last two years?"

"Definitely. What's not to enjoy?"

"We've grown close, and it's meant a lot to me to get to know you. There's some other stuff, too. It is not enough to be loved in this world. You have to be able to love, too. If you don't, you'll miss out on much of what life has to offer."

Natalie shrugged. "You love me. My parents loved me. They didn't get me, but they loved me as best they could."

How to explain this to her? "As I've said before, we're different, you and me. Different isn't wrong or bad, just different. Harder. And with being different comes the onus to explain that difference, how it feels, and to help others understand. Did you do that with your parents?"

Natalie squirmed. "They were the adults. The onus should be on them, right?"

"Partly. But as you got older, some of the responsibility rested on your shoulders to help them understand. They'd be in a better position to help you if you did that."

"It's moot now. They're back in San Diego, and I'm here. Doesn't matter anymore. I'll probably never see them again."

"Never say never."

Part III

Part III

Chapter Forty-Five

Present Day

"I thought you couldn't cross the border; it was too risky." This made no sense to Natalie that Alejandro planned to go to San Diego.

"I'll risk it just this once."

"But we're fine here. Why would you want to go there?"

"You need to see your parents. Make peace with them."

"Who cares? I certainly don't, and they'll have gotten over me by now."

Alejandro shook his head. "No, I doubt that. They'll be missing you and be hurt that you've not been in touch. They worry."

"How could you know that?"

"Study, Nat, study. Pay attention to your courses, on how people interact. Trust me, Barbara and Howard love you and want to see you."

Oh, how his life had changed since Natalie came into

his care. No longer did he live for himself, other than setting money aside for his brother and mother. He owed Natalie much more.

Both her parents' cars were in the driveway. Natalie wiped her palms on the thighs of her jeans. She studied the place that had been her home for less than a year, the place her parents claimed would be their fresh start.

It had been a new start, at least for her, and not in the way Barbara and Howard had intended.

Why was she still standing here? She glanced back at the darkened windows of the car where her father, her *real* father waited. The rat had insisted she go into the house on her own, have a few minutes with her parents by herself. Is that what a good dad would do? Shouldn't he be willing to support her?

They'd been through this. Although Alejandro could be indulgent with some things, with many things, there were times where his will was iron and nothing Natalie did could budge him.

He had this thing about teaching her. Facing her parents alone was one of those things, he'd said.

He also tried to make her analyze herself. Sheesh. Who wanted to be bothered doing that? She'd made it these last 18 years just fine without psychoanalyzing herself. It was pointless. She was who she was, and everyone could take her or leave her. Who cared?

Somehow, something inside her did care. Was that why her palms felt sweaty, her heart rate a little faster than normal? Never had she been nervous with these people, her adoptive parents. She knew they loved and supported her, no matter what, even when they didn't understand the first thing about her.

This was ridiculous. This was so not who she was. What did she care what anyone thought of her? She could blow them off easily, and she had money. She didn't need them.

With a deep, fortifying breath, Natalie strode to the door, opening it as if she had every right to do so. Once inside, she let the door close as quietly as possible, then stood there listening.

From the kitchen came the sound of her parents' voices, both of them testy with each other. That much hadn't changed, and it gave her courage to enter the room. "I thought once I was out of the way you guys would get along better."

Stunned, Barbara froze mid-sentence.

Howard rose from his crouch under the sink to gaze at the child he'd not seen in two years.

Barbara rushed to her daughter, with her arms open. Something in Natalie's look stopped her just two feet away without touching. Even as a small child, Natalie had never been affectionate. Barbara respected that, even though she'd prefer to wrap this child of her heart in her arms and hold her tight. "How did you get here? We're so happy to see you!"

"My father brought me."

Howard flinched at her words.

Noticing, Natalie smiled at him. "Hi, dad." Alejandro would be proud of her for reading the situation and responding with what people might want.

She was rewarded by the huge grin splitting Howard's face. "My baby girl." Turning to his wife, "She's come home, Barb."

"Not really," began Natalie, then stopped.

A toddler entered the room. "Who dat?" he asked.

Howard picked up the little boy. "This is your big sister, Natalie. You were just a baby the last time you saw her."

"Nat, come in, come. Let's get you something to eat. Want coffee?"

"Sure."

"Sorry we're in a bit of a disarray here. Howard and I are just cleaning up, getting ready for the new tenants to move in on the first of the month."

"Tenants? You don't live here?"

"Ah, no." Her parents looked at each other. "Natalie, you see, we've been living apart. Howard has an apartment on 45th Street, and Liam and I rent a little house a few blocks away."

"Why?"

Howard tried to explain. "Things were tough after you left. We did a lot of blaming of ourselves and each other. We weren't getting along, so we separated, renting out this place."

"Was it because of me?" Why should she feel guilty for their decisions? They were adults and could do what they want. Somehow, though, she suspected that their marital problems were partly her fault. Geez, was Alejandro rubbing off on her? There was a time when she wouldn't have cared how anyone else was doing. It was easier that way.

Liam squirmed to get down. As soon as his father set him on the floor, the child went to Natalie, holding up his arms.

Trying not to feel self-conscious, Natalie picked him up, settling him awkwardly against her left hip. Wow, the kid was a lot heavier than when he'd been six months old. He was kind of cute.

Liam wound his hands through strands of Natalie's long hair, lifting them, then watching them drop back into position. "Pretty." Then he patted her cheeks gently with both hands.

Outside, a commotion caught their attention.

[illegible faded text at top of page]

Chapter Forty-Six

Hoping he'd given them enough time to meet each other, Alejandro got out of his car. While sitting behind the tinted windows of the rental was risky, this was the worst part, walking to the house in plain sight. It had to be done, though. Waiting simply delayed the inevitable. You did what you had to do.

Damn! Wouldn't you know it?

The door of the house next door flew up and out tumbled Amy, the child they'd snatched two years ago.

Lowering his head and putting his hand to his face, Alejandro continued up the driveway.

"Mommy! Mommy!" Amy stopped quickly. "Mommy, it's him, that man who had me in the hotel room and gave me that red juice."

From the front door, Cynthia stuck her head out. Her shock only lasted seconds before instinct took over. Racing to her daughter, she snatched Amy, shielding her body with her own. Her eyes not leaving Alejandro's form, she yelled, "Boyd! It's that man. It's Alejandro. He's here!"

"Get Amy to Elizabeth's house. Lock yourselves in with the kids. Phone Brandon and tell him I need backup."

He didn't have much time. Alejandro opened the door to the kitchen and took in the scene before him. A scene that cut to his heart, yet it was what he wanted for his daughter. Holding her little brother in her arms. Her parents looking at her with love.

Yet they regarded him with loathing and fear. Howard took Liam from Natalie's arms, passing him to Barbara, then he pulled Nat closer, placing her between him and his wife.

"We meet again," Alejandro began. He glanced at the commotion outside. He had a lot to say in a short amount of time. "Look. Natalie needs you. That's why we're here. She needs a sanctum, a safe place, a family to guide her."

Howard put his arm around Natalie's shoulders.

Alejandro swallowed. These people belonged together. Natalie had only been on loan to him temporarily. Maybe long enough for him to learn what he needed to help her. "I know you loved Natalie and did your best. But there are things you don't understand. Stuff that comes naturally to most kids doesn't for her; it never did. You know she struggled as a child and there are reasons why.

"You can help her now, especially now that she's an adult. She needs a code to live by. Teach her what's allowed and what is not acceptable but explain why. It might feel like stating the obvious, but it has to be done if she's to have a good life, the kind you'd want for her."

Car doors slammed outside.

"She's started college and is doing okay. She needs to continue, especially in the subjects she's taking. She needs to understand people and will need your help with that. There's money for her education and to give her a good start in life. She can run my business, if she so chooses later on." He held up his hand as Howard started to interrupt. "My *legitimate* business, nothing shady or illegal about it." He continued, talking faster now. "This house is now paid for and in your names. There's a college fund set up for your son, as well as a living allowance for all of you. I thank you for looking after my daughter and loving her as your own."

The door yanked open behind him, and three uniformed officers filled the room.

Alejandro nodded his head at Natalie, locking eyes with Howard. "Get her out of here. She doesn't need to see this. And take care of her. Please."

Catching on, Howard put his arms around his wife, son, and daughter, leading them from the room.

"Alejandro Ramirez, you are under arrest for…"

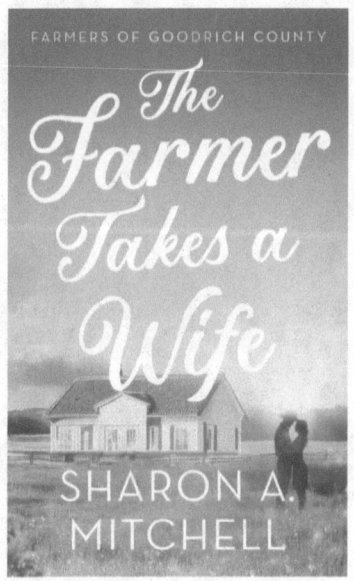

The Farmer Takes a Wife: Chapter One

Google Maps lied. Who can you trust if not Google? The pleasant voice insisted that she leave the highway and take this secondary road. Road? Who would call it that? Not a speck of pavement in sight. There was gravel in places, but she'd left those spots far behind.

The fates were against her. Even her weather app told her a fib. It promised sunny skies, so where did this rain come from? To be fair, this was no longer technically rain, but more like a foggy drizzle.

The map said her destination was only ten miles away. That was 40 minutes ago.

Mona hated when that "poor me" refrain entered her head. She resolutely shoved it away, like always. Whining never changed things for her. Just get on with it. If it has to be done, it has to be done.

Still….

Shifting in her seat, she gripped the steering wheel tighter. Head and shoulders tilted forward. Hands at a perfect ten and two position or take out the "a" at "Hands at perfect ten ..." That meant she was in full control of her vehicle. Right?

She skidded across the surface into the other lane. Or what would have been a lane if anything was marked on this rutted, mud-drenched excuse for a road. No wonder she'd not seen a single car in the last half hour. Who in their right mind would drive here? At least she'd avoid a smash-up since she was in the only car on a horizon that stretched endlessly.

Steer into the skid; she thought that's what they'd taught in driver's training. Or was that just for snow? Cars weren't built for mud, at least hers certainly wasn't.

She was getting used to slipping her way down the road, traveling at less than 20 miles per hour. Anything above that, and she felt the imminent loss of control. She'd make it. Slow and steady, just like her life. Only small corrections required to stay the course. Didn't matter if she enjoyed the journey; this was her path.

But that was all about the change. Her new life started now, or as soon as she traversed the next bend or two and finally arrived.

Whoa! No, no, no!

Mona's clenched fists squeezed the plastic wheel until her grip slipped. She moved her sweating palms, one at a time, to find a drier purchase. Wished she could take the time to wipe her hands on her jeans.

No! Steering into the skid helped the little Ford Focus go where it wanted to go. Yanking the wheel the other way, the car clung to the left side of the road, narrowly missing toppling into the ditch. But she yanked too hard, and now battled to keep all four tires on the semblance of what might once have been gravel, not in the right-hand ditch.

Okay, okay, you can do this, she told herself. Over and

over. You're fine. Almost there. The endless Great Plains landscape seemed to tell her to keep believing that. Nothing but fields stretching from here to eternity, or at least as she glimpsed through the fog. No civilization in sight.

Willing herself to relax, she took a second to use the back of a hand to brush the bangs out of her eyes. It was fine. She was again in the middle of this lonely road. She risked removing her left hand from the steering wheel to rub it on her thigh, flex her fingers, and then did the same with her right. Couldn't be much farther. Consciously, she willed her shoulders to relax, and unclenched her jaw.

She could feel some of the tension drain away. Deep breaths. Just hold on.

Between one deep breath and another, things changed. Overhead, the clouds roiled. What now seemed a friendly drizzle turned into a torrent of rain, blinding, obscuring the road, turning the ground beneath her tires into an oozing, churning quagmire.

The skids came non-stop now, every inch a fight to stay on the road. Why had she ever thought she could do this?

Quit it. Of course, you can. Just concentrate. You'll be out of this mess soon.

She huffed a breath upward to blow her bangs from her eyes. Why hadn't she taken the time for a haircut before leaving town?

Up ahead, was there something? It looked like a grove of trees, maybe planted in a line. The first sign of human interference in this world she found herself in. Hard to tell with the driving rain, but it looked like there might be build-ings behind the trees. Maybe a farm site. That had to be a sign that she was approaching the town.

No! It was happening again, sliding from one side of the road to the other, fighting the wheel to make it obey her will. This time it was even harder as the increased rain turned the mud into a stew flowing into the bumps and ruts, snagging her tires, fighting her for control of the car.

Whoa! Too far to the left, almost in the ditch. Mona wrenched the wheel, desperate to wrestle the little car back into the center of the lane.

Too much, she pulled too hard. Now the mud pitched her to the far right. From the corner of her eye, she saw what looked like an approach, maybe an entrance into some farmyard. Surely no one would mind if she pulled in and parked to wait out the storm.

Yanking the wheel, she tried to make the approach. At the same time, her foot slipped, hitting the gas pedal. That instant burst of speed got a vote of approval from the mud. Together, the two things propelled her past the entrance, toward the end of a metal culvert sticking out of the ditch.

There was no correcting this skid; it all happened too fast. One second, she was on the road, the next a tire caught and spun her around, the left side pitching into the ditch. With a lurch, the culvert caught the front bumper, sending the car jerking forward. Mona's head connected first with the driver's side window, then the steering wheel. She thought she heard someone's horn honking, then nothing.

The Farmer Takes a Wife: Chapter Two

One thing was a given with cattle - they expected to get fed, no matter what.

Much as he'd prefer to put his feet up and stay inside, he had a farm to run, and right now, that meant getting hay bales to the cows. At least the tractor's heater and defroster worked. Sort of. He used the side of his hand to clear a spot on the window the defroster never quite seemed to reach. The grips on the tractor tires churned in the mud. His yard would be a mess once things dried up, and he'd have to work to smooth out the ruts. Again.

Taking aim, and increasing the throttle slightly, Reid Manson shoved the prongs jutting out from the front of his tractor into the large, round bale, lifting it into the air, and backing up. Wheeling almost from motor memory, he peered through the pounding rain in the direction of the pasture. You'd never know it now, but it had been a drought-like year, with the grass drying up, producing little in the way of useful feed for the cattle. They needed their grazing supplemented with these bales.

Yep, they saw him and now all hundred and fifty animals turned toward where they knew he'd set down the bale. Creatures of habit. Sort of like Reid. That was okay. Habits became comfortable. They got things done. Nothing wrong with the predictable.

Mostly he wore baseball caps when out working, but in weather like this, nothing beat a Stetson. His was shaped just right and would send the water down the back of his rain slicker, instead of his neck. The wide front brim would keep the rain out of his eyes.

He sat for a second, dreading the next part. How often had he done this? Almost daily since he'd been old enough to reach the pedals on this old tractor. Get over it, Reid. Just get it done. With a sigh, he throttled back, and shifted the levers into neutral and park, and pushed the hat more firmly on his head. He'd lost one a time or two when the wind took it. Not today. Today the plan was to get chores done as quickly as possible, then settle down with a bowl of the fiery chili bubbling right now in the slow cooker.

Half-standing, he leaned over and worked the latch on the tractor door. He kept meaning to take the latch apart and oil it well, but somehow, other tasks snagged his time. If you grabbed the stupid latch just right, it worked, but who could count on perfection all the time? Only times like now, when he was in a hurry, did the finicky latch truly irk him and he'd promise himself once again to fix it tomorrow.

But he got it, like he always did, and lowered himself down the ladder, holding onto his hat as he went. Yep, that wind wanted his hat, but not as much as Reid did.

Pulling the knife from his pocket, Reid entered the circle of milling cattle to cut the strings on the ~~hay~~ bale so the animals could pull at the hay more easily.

What was that? So used to his yard, Reid knew every

sound - every clatter and rattle of buildings and machinery, the call of every bird and mammal that claimed the area as home.

But that sound reminded him more of being in a city, the endless traffic and senseless honking of horns. He stopped and peered in the direction of the road.

Was that a light? Hard to tell in the rain. Well, whatever it was, could wait. He had cattle to tend to, then a supper calling his name.

Three more bales should do it. Following his tracks back to the bale yard got harder each time as the tractor tires churned through the mud and ruts they'd created on the last trip.

Done. He got out of the tractor one final time to shut the gate. It was still there, that noise. Now that the rain was easing off somewhat, yeah, it did look like a light. And honking.

He climbed back into the tractor, ready to idle it to cool down the turbo chargers before shutting it down. Should he? He'd done enough for one day and would be up at sunrise tomorrow. Should he ignore that sound? Could he?

Clenching his teeth, he throttled the tractor back up to operating speed. No way was he walking out to the road in this rain to check. He steered the machine the rest of the way through his yard, aiming for the gate. Yeah, he was making a mess of his road, but he'd deal with that tomor- row. Just one more thing.

Closer now, he could see it, only one headlight visible above the ditch. A car, one of those little things he doubted any normal-sized human being could fit into. One tire sat atop the side of his culvert. The rear tire sank into the quagmire at the side of the road, while the two left tires were in the ditch. The tiny vehicle canted at an angle, more off the road than on. The horn blew non-stop.

Not bothering to secure his hat, he slammed the levers out of gear and jumped out of the tractor. Instantly, the wind snatched his Stetson and made off with it. Brackish, frigid water slopped over the tops of his boots as he leaped into the ditch to yank open the driver's side door.

Both cold wind and rain rushed in through the opened door, causing the woman to breathe a faint protest. She lifted a hand to her head. "Ouch, that hurts."

Ah, yeah, it probably would. Reid used his coat sleeve to wipe away part of the trail of blood trickling down her cheek.

The woman flinched back.

"Sorry, did I hurt you?"

"No, it startled me. Guess I'm jumpy after this." She gestured around her car. "Where am I?"

Good grief. Did the woman have amnesia? "You're about three miles outside the town of Goodrich."

"I almost made it then."

Not many people came to Goodrich; it was mainly a place for locals. The only new people were schoolteachers, but this was April. A new flock of teachers wouldn't appear until late summer. "You were looking for Goodrich? Why didn't you take the highway?"

"Blame it on Siri. She steered me wrong. The map said this road was the shortest route."

"Maybe. Under ideal conditions, that is. You may have noticed; this is not ideal driving weather."

"Yeah, I figured that out."

"I don't think we can do much about your car tonight."

Mona looked at the ditch and the road. "Is there a hotel around here where I can stay?"

Reid snorted. Where did she think she was? "You do know that Goodrich is just a small town, don't you?"

"I realize that."

Okay. Few small towns had Holiday Inns, at least in this part of the country. Maybe she hit her head harder than he thought. "Are you feeling all right? Looks like you have a goose egg starting on your forehead."

She touched the bump gingerly with her fingertips. "It hurts, but it's not bad."

"You're bleeding." Although it had slowed already.

"I'm fine." She paused. "I, ah, wonder if I could bother you for a ride. I know the weather is horrid, but I need to find a place to stay for the night. I thought I'd spend the first night in a hotel, until I could check things out, but if that won't work, I have a house I can go to."

Images of his chili, along with a crusty loaf of French bread, played in his mind, but he dismissed them. "Sure, I can give you a ride. Whose place are you going to?"

"It was my grandmother's. Lily McAllister. Do you know her?"

Sure. Everyone knew Lily McAllister, Reid recalled. She was a fixture around town in her day, organizing and cooking for every fall supper and community get together. At least she had. It had been years since Old Lady McAllister had been up to much.

At first, when people noticed she was slipping, they took turns checking up on her. People drove her to medical appointments, brought her meals, looked after her yard, and helped with the housekeeping. When she would let them, that is. After all, she'd looked after the town most of her adult life, and she was alone. No family around to see to her, other than her neighbors and friends. Finally, well-meaning townsfolk got together and moved her into the old folks' home. From there, it wasn't long after a number of short hospital admissions, that she passed away. The grocery store had a collection pot at the till; everyone pitched in to give Old Lady McAllister a proper farewell and burial.

There had been no family members in attendance. "You say Lily was your grandmother?" His tone dripped ice; he could not abide those who shirked their obligations and looking after family was at the top of his list of responsibilities.

"Yes. My father's mother."

Reid's eyes narrowed. "And where were you and your father when Lily needed you?"

The Farmer Takes a Wife: Chapter Three

Mona recoiled at the tone in the man's voice. Sure, they were meeting under unusual circumstances, but she thought farm folk were supposed to be friendly. Or maybe it was her perceptions that were off. She thought he'd been friendly, or at least neutral, when he first yanked open her door. Why the chill now? Was something off about this guy?

It suddenly dawned on her just how alone and vulnerable she was. The only person around was this man whose mood seemed changeable. No one knew where she was. Sure, her parents had a vague idea, but they'd made it clear that if she left, she was on her own.

Glancing at the passenger seat, she wondered if she could edge over the console and climb into the other seat, at least putting a few feet between her and the scowling guy who blocked the only other exit from her car.

She pulled back as he leaned in, frowning at her face.

"Are you sure you're okay? Need to go to the hospital?"

With him? You've got to be kidding. Mona shook her

head, then wished she hadn't. A low moan escaped her. She must have hit her head harder than she'd thought.

Suddenly, the guy reached in, his broad shoulders filling the entire escape route left by the opened door. Reaching across, he undid her seatbelt. He put one arm behind her, and the other he shoved under her legs and tugged.

"Hey! What are you doing?" There was nowhere to go to get away from his presence or his grasping hands. His head touched hers and she could smell his shampoo, something apple-like.

"I'm trying to get you out of here. Unless you want to spend the night in your car."

Then his arms tightened, and he pulled, then lifted. She was free of the car. The man stumbled slightly as he compensated for her weight on the uneven ground and the water beneath his feet.

Instinctively, she put her arms around his neck, then realized what she was doing. "You can put me down now."

"Here in this puddle? I don't think you want that." He took broad strides that carried them up the bank of the ditch and onto the road. Here, the footing wasn't much better as he slid through the mud.

"Where are you taking me?" She kicked her legs in an attempt to break free of his grasp.

"Hold still. You don't want me to drop you in this."

He had a point. She ducked her head to keep the rain from her eyes. Then they were at this monstrous green machine. The man turned sideways and placed her feet on the steps.

"Grasp the sides of the ladder with your hands," he instructed. "Now climb up."

She did as she was told. Then he crowded up behind her, his front pressed uncomfortably close to her back as he reached around her to open the door. He pulled her back towards him, out of the way so the door could open fully. "Get in."

In? Where? The cab was too small for two people. Again, the guy pressed far too close to her, doing something to the arm of the seat, then he pushed past her to sit behind the steering wheel.

"Sit," he ordered, nodding to the wide, padded arm he'd lowered to seat level.

Sit? There? Right up against him?

"Or stand if you'd prefer. But better hang on to something."

With a roar, the tractor started up. He pushed levers, gave a quick glance over his shoulder behind them, then the thing lurched as it began to move. Self-preservation had Mona grabbing for the first thing her fingers touched in order to remain upright. That happened to be his shoulder. As if burned, she jerked back, her other hand seeking purchase. The only thing within her grasp was the steering wheel.

"Hey! Don't grab that!" The man quickly regained control of the tractor before all the tires left the lane. "If we get stuck here, it'll take hours to get out."

Mona braced herself with one hand on the rear window and the other on the bar of the door behind her. As the tractor skidded through the mud, her grip tightened. Suddenly, the door opened, and she was falling.

A quick hand grabbed the front of her shirt, preventing her from tumbling to the ground, probably under the enormous wheels. "Don't touch the door latch unless you mean to get out of the machine." Tentatively, his fist released its stranglehold on her sweatshirt. "Are you okay?"

She nodded, although she was pretty sure her heart had never beaten such a frantic tattoo.

With one foot depressing the clutch and the other on the brake, he kept one steadying hand on her waist while reaching behind her to pull the door shut. "You might want to sit down. It's easier to keep your balance than standing." He edged over in his seat, to the right, giving her some room. Not much, but maybe a quarter of the seat.

Without looking at him, she lowered herself to the five-inch arm rest, trying to keep her hips from spreading too far onto the seat, from touching him. Useless endeavor. The first pothole the front tire dipped into threw her against her seat mate, her right side plastered to his left.

He ignored her. Well, if he could pretend this forced proximity wasn't happening, so could she. But perching this way felt rickety, and she so didn't want to end up in his lap the next time the tires fell into another rut. Mona placed her right arm along the back of the tractor seat, gripping the edge with her fingers. There. That felt more secure. Then the tractor slid again, throwing their bodies into even closer contact. Of its own volition, her arm left the seat back to cling to the broad shoulders of the man beside her. Recoiling, she loosened her grip. "Sorry," she said, returning her arm to the seat back. That way, there was at least half an inch between her and the back of this stranger.

A stranger who smelled good. Where did that thought come from? Yeah, they were trapped together in this metal and glass microcosm of the universe, protected from the elements, but not from each other.

Outside, the rain beat on the roof and windows, barely discernible above the rumble of the giant machine. The floor was slick with mud from the guy's boots, mud and likely other stuff she didn't want to think about. Her nose tried to categorize the many scents that crept in - the aroma of damp clothing, the hint of barnyard, that apple scent, and something else, something male.

Dragging her thoughts back from such extraneous things, she centered on the most important. "Where are we going?"

The guy pointed ahead of them. "To the house."

Now, she could make out the shape of a building ahead. White with a green roof and trim - an older house, maybe from the 60s or so. Not too different from the house where she'd grown up. "Who lives here?"

He looked at her with one brow lowered. "I do."

Well, that was obvious. "Anyone else, I mean?"

"No, I live alone."

Now, wasn't that just peachy?

Grab your copy...
vinci-books.com/TakesAWife

About the Author

Sharon A. Mitchell lives on a farm, with her nearest neighbor several miles away. Does that seem like a setting to spark the imagination? It does for her.

When she's not writing her numerous thriller series, she can be found taking long walks with her hundred-pound German Shepherd dogs, Pickles and Dill. (She didn't name them - don't blame her.)

www.ingramcontent.com/pod-product-compliance
Lightning Source LLC
Chambersburg PA
CBHW011426010726
47494CB00011B/2515

* 9 7 8 1 0 3 6 7 0 7 5 6 9 *